Absolutely swept away by Julia Green's new book *To the Edge of the World* . . . a wonderful read. **Gill Lewis**

A quietly lovely book full of birds and boats and faraway places. It reminded me of the joy of exploration, and why I love the Scottish Isles. **Sally Nicholls**

Just finished Julia's wonderful story and, as I expected, absolutely adored It's such a lovely story of facing our fears and daring to be different. loved the world she's created—the nature imagery, the sea, the family dynamics—definitely the work of an exceptional writer! I think ngo is fast becoming my favourite fictional dog! **Emma Carroll**

this story about identity, friendship and becoming yourself has everything: real adventure, real danger all set in a real place, with the wonder of a magical realm, plus an irresistible dog! A story as clear and powerful as an Atlantic wave. **Nicola Davies**

It's been a real treat to read *To the Edge of the World* by the brilliant Julia Green. It's her best book yet! **David Almond**

A powerful story, vivid and evocative; one that raises some really interesting questions for young people about how to live and what to hope for. **Lucy Christopher**

Dear Reader

Do you fancy setting out on a wild sea adventure to the edge of the world? Feeling the wind in your hair and the salt sea on your lips, and heading off beyond the horizon? Of course you do! So come on then, let's go . . .

What's that? You can't actually go right now? You would *love* to—it's just that you have homework to do—and it's nearly tea-time—and you're feeling a bit tired—and you've got to be up early for school in the morning—and honestly, you can't just take off like that. Maybe one day . . .

That's how I feel a lot of the time—which is one of the reasons why I really fell in love with *To the Edge of the World*. Julia Green writes so compellingly about Jamie and Mara and Django the dog, and about the wild places they explore, that I could really feel I was there with them on the open seas and remote islands. Safe on my sofa,

I could share every heartbeat of their adventure—the danger and the uncertainty, but also the exhilaration and the amazing sense of freedom. If, like me, you love the wild outdoors and dream of adventure, then this is definitely the book for you.

So curl up in your favourite reading spot and let yourself be whisked away by a master storyteller. You'll have a wonderful adventure and perhaps you'll be inspired, too—to fight for your true freedom like Mara, to face your fears like Jamie, to find out who you really want to be—and of course to plan your own adventures . . .

Liz Cross
Head of Children's Publishing
Oxford University Press

For David

OXFORD
UNIVERSITY PRESS

Great Clarendon Street, Oxford OX2 6DP

Oxford University Press is a department of the University of Oxford.
It furthers the University's objective of excellence in research, scholarship,
and education by publishing worldwide. Oxford is a registered trade mark of
Oxford University Press in the UK and in certain other countries

British Library Cataloguing in Publication Data

Data available

ISBN: 978-0-19-275845-3

1 3 5 7 9 10 8 6 4 2

Printed in Great Britain
Paper used in the production of this book is a natural,
recyclable product made from wood grown in sustainable forests.
The manufacturing process conforms to the environmental
regulations of the country of origin.

To
the
Edge
of the
World

JULIA GREEN

OXFORD
UNIVERSITY PRESS

Contents

Imagine a tiny island far out in the Atlantic ocean off the west coast of Scotland. It's joined by causeway bridges top and bottom to other small islands, part of the archipelago called the Outer Hebrides. On some days, you can hardly see where the sea ends and the land begins, everything merged in a blue-grey mist of sea spray and wind-blown sand.

This is where I live now.

There is nothing between here and America.

I say nothing, but what I mean, of course, is nothing but ocean. And about sixty-five kilometres out to sea, one last remote outcrop of islands and sea stacks, with the highest sea cliffs anywhere in the UK: St Kilda.

The islands at the edge of the world.

Before, we lived in the grey city on the mainland, and I hated school and was miserable. But Mum grew up on this island. She told us stories about it. We visited Grandpa and Granny in their house overlooking the sea. And then a house nearby came up for sale, and we bought it.

We moved in spring. Mum got a job in the fisheries' processing place, so she stinks of fish all the time but she's happy again. Like me, she hated living in the city. Dad had to stay in Glasgow during the week so he could carry on doing his job, so we only saw him every other weekend, and only then if the ferry was running and the sea wasn't too rough for landing. My sister Fee (Fiona, she's thirteen) missed all her friends, especially Megan. She'd tell you a different story about living here. But this is about me, and what happened that first summer. My name is Jamie Mackinnon.

Everyday life on our island still depends on tides, and sea states, and wind directions, and storms. In a city, you never think about those things. But here, a high tide combined with a sudden storm surge is so dangerous that people can die. People do die.

I think about things like these a lot: tides and currents and death by drowning. That's my worst fear. The sea is beautiful but it is also deadly.

Part One:
How it Started

The Girl

It was Monday, early morning. July. No one else was up. For once, it wasn't raining. This was one of the rare bright, brilliant days when the sky is an arc of blue and the sea turns turquoise and the sand gleams silver-white, and it looks like a tropical paradise island. It IS paradise, just much colder.

I ran down to the beach nearest our house. I do that most mornings in the holidays. I don't go in the sea, ever, but I love being the first person to step on the new-washed sand. If you're quiet, sometimes you can see an otter on its way between land and sea.

The tide was just going down. It was an extra high tide—called a spring tide even in summer—because of the full moon. The tide had left the usual line of stuff—seaweed and plastic rubbish, shells and a ridge of pebbles, bits of fishing net and an old shoe. My feet sank into the damp sand.

I stopped running.

Someone else had been here.

A trail of footprints tracked along next to the tideline.

I made my own footprints next to them. My trainers left a pattern of ridges and diamond shapes. The others were smaller and narrower, with the faint print of toes and heel.

Bare feet. Someone small and light.

Now I saw paw prints, too—not otter, more likely dog. Scuffed sand, the whispery marks where maybe a tail had dragged along.

I scanned the beach for the owner of the feet, but the whole wide stretch of the beach was empty.

Who else had been down here this early?

I followed the tracks to see where they went. The beach is huge: miles of silver-white sand. I ran and it felt amazing because of the sun and the glittering sea. White birds called arctic terns dive-bombed me to keep me off their nesting places at the pebbly top edge of the beach, so I was dodging and ducking and after a while not really thinking about the footprints any more. I found a grey pebble with crystals of quartz, and a tiny sea-scoured bird skull. I put them in my pocket.

A flapping sound made me look out to sea. Sound carries long distances over water. A small dinghy with a white sail was trying to turn—tack—and the sail flapped as it lost the wind. For a second it looked like the boat might tip right over. I stopped to watch, my heart thudding.

There was a moment of pause, like someone taking a breath, and then the sail stopped flapping and stretched out smooth as the wind filled it, and the boat righted itself and sailed on. The sun glinted off the white stern, and lit up the person steering so I could see who it was.

A girl all by herself, except for a dog, perched now on the bow of the boat, and she was sailing the dinghy as if she had done it all her life. She didn't look any older than me.

I carried on running along the beach, she sailed, both of us going in parallel, with the sea between us. The dog barked and barked. It wagged its tail. It watched me. And then the boat speeded up, scudded along and left me way behind.

The girl never looked at me once. Her focus was the sail, and the wind, and the water.

And then, she disappeared. Sailed right round the bay and out of sight, beyond the line of rocks. I stared until my eyes watered, watching for the boat to come back.

I waited for ages. The tide went further out. The light changed. I found a stick and drew pictures in the sand. A boat with sails. A dog. I wrote my name in big letters—JAMIE—and then I scrubbed it out again with my foot. I drew a massive whale, the proper size. Still no sign of the girl in the boat. The sea was choppy further out: white-edged waves on navy blue. I imagined being out there alone; all that water, deep under the boat. I shuddered. An extra big gust of wind . . . I imagined the boat tipping . . . the girl falling overboard. Did anyone know she was out there? Anyone but me?

I zigzagged back along the beach, following the footsteps in the damp sand. Mine and the girl's.

I thought about her: the confident way she sailed her boat, how free and wild and fearless she looked. She wasn't one of the girls at my new school. She wasn't anyone I'd seen on the island before.

Who was she?

Back at our house, I kicked off my sandy trainers and left them in the porch.

Mum was in the kitchen, shoving clothes into the washing machine.

'Hello, early bird!' she said. 'Find anything good on the beach?'

I shook my head. I poured cereal into a bowl and slopped in some milk and shovelled it down.

'What will you do today while I'm at work?' Mum clicked on the kettle. She put bread into the toaster.

'Help Grandpa at the boat shed,' I said.

'Good,' Mum said. 'Come back for lunch.' She put two mugs on the table. 'I'm sorry it has to be like this.'

'Like what?'

'You and Fee, left to your own devices so much. I wish I could spend more time with you. But I have to work.'

'It's fine,' I said. 'Stop worrying.'

'And Grandpa and Granny are there, if you need anything.'

'Yes.'

'So, be good. Don't go into the sea by yourself.'

'No way I'm swimming in that sea,' I said.

Mum laughed. 'I know, it's freezing.' She poured water into the teapot.

She doesn't know the real reason. How much I think about the danger. The deep water.

Fee clomped down the stairs. She flumped down at the table with a massive sigh.

I wasn't going to stay around to listen to her moaning.

'Got to go,' I said. 'Bye, Mum.'

The Boat Shed

Tap tap tap. The rhythmic sounds of a hammer bounced off the stone walls of the row of houses near the harbour and echoed across the bay.

I cycled down the bumpy track to the boat shed with its red tin roof.

Grandpa waved through the open door.

I leaned my bike against the shed wall and stepped though the doorway. It seemed dark in the shed at first. Gradually my eyes adjusted. I wrinkled my nose at the smell: hot metal, new wood. Dust.

Grandpa nodded to me. 'Morning, Jamie.'

'Hello, Grandpa.' I watched him pick up the hand plane and

with both hands move it steadily along the top edge of a plank of wood. Paper-thin wood-shavings fell in gold curls onto the floor at his feet. The new boat was taking shape: light from the big back window danced over the wooden hull.

I knew not to talk when Grandpa worked. He has to concentrate really hard. He does it all by eye, just a few measurements scribbled down on a bit of old paper. The island boats have been built like this for generations, the craft and skill handed down from father to son. Only Grandpa didn't have a son, just one daughter, Kathleen. That's my mum. And she didn't want to learn to build boats.

But I do. 'Watch and learn,' Grandpa had said. 'See how you go. Find out if you have a feel for it.'

That July morning, I sat on a pile of sacks and watched Grandpa at work: his hands on the wood, and the way he braced his body and planted his feet strong and square. I breathed in deep the smell of new wood and dust and salt and fish. Through the big window at the back of the shed I could see the curve of the bay, the bright red and green buoys that mark the harbour entrance. A fishing boat chugged in with its wake of screaming gulls. A sudden strong stench of fish came as the hatches were opened and emptied.

I waited for Grandpa to have a break.

He laid the tools on the bench and poured tea from a dusty flask. He nodded at me. 'Ready to help?'

'Yes.'

'You can sweep up, first. Tidy the place a bit. Broom's over there.'

I'd hoped he'd let me use the plane. I liked the way it sliced along the edge, sending up the curl of wood before it. But I knew there was no point saying that to Grandpa. One mistake, and I might waste a whole plank. The wood was expensive: larch that had to be ordered from Europe and brought in on the ferry from the mainland.

He sipped his tea.

'I saw this girl, sailing a boat with a white sail in the bay. By herself,' I said. 'A girl with a scruffy dog. Early this morning . . .'

'Ah,' Grandpa said, and he sighed. 'That'll be the wild lass. Roams about the island. Sails her boat. Esther, the mother's called. I've forgotten what they call the child.'

'She doesn't go to our school,' I said. 'I've never seen her before.'

'They're a law unto themselves, that pair. Scratch a living

9

from the sea—flotsam and jetsam made into knick-knacks to sell to gullible visitors.'

'What's gullible mean?'

'Taken in, by a load of nonsense. Pebbles painted like creatures and birds. People will buy that kind of tat when they're in the holiday mood. But the girl can handle a boat, I'll give her that. I've seen her out there.' He nodded his head towards the bay, framed by the boat shed window.

'Where does she live?' I asked.

'Out on the western shore with her mother. They keep to themselves. Don't come to the church or the community hall. I've seen the woman but we've never spoken. There's island gossip—the way she hides herself away, like she's run away from something—but that's just tittle.' Grandpa stood to stretch out his back. He screwed the cap back on the tea flask. 'Back to work, Jamie.'

He planed the next plank; I swept the shavings into piles and carried them to the bin. The shed was warm and smelled sweet. I thought of all the generations of people who had made boats here. My family on this island, stretching back and back. I love that. It makes me feel like I *belong* here.

Grandpa says his boat design is much the same as the Vikings used over a thousand years ago. His boats are *clinker-built*, which means the wooden frame is covered with planks which overlap each other slightly and form shallow steps, rather than the hull being completely smooth. The design specially suits the tricky seas around here and the boats are easy to handle under sail or oars. They are particularly good for lobster fishing around the dangerous reefs on the Atlantic west coast. Grandpa's own boat is the *Kathleen Mary*.

Grandpa must have still been thinking about the girl. 'We should teach you to sail, soon, Jamie,' he said. 'First, you must get stronger as a swimmer.'

I didn't say anything. I didn't tell him how scared I am of the sea. I didn't want anyone to know that.

Grandpa fitted the next curved rib. He handed me a small off-cut of larch wood. 'Try the chisel, see what it can do, how to shape the edge.'

My first cuts went too deep. It was hard to control the chisel so it shaved rather than sliced. I cut the palm of my left hand when it slipped. I didn't show Grandpa. I pressed my hand against my jeans until the blood stopped. It hurt like mad at first.

At lunchtime Grandpa slid the big door shut and padlocked it and we walked back home together. I pushed my bike. We went along the single-track road, past the small lochan which has a tiny island with a few spindly trees on it. The only place that trees can grow is where they are out of the reach of sheep. They nibble off everything, every tiny seedling. Some people would like to get rid of the sheep altogether. Over time it would change the landscape completely. But for now, there are no big trees anywhere on our island. And that's why the larch and oak for boatbuilding has to come from the mainland and beyond.

I thought about how watery this island is: more water than land. There are sea lochs, which are tidal, and freshwater ones, like this one, which are not. If you look at a proper map, you see all this blue and hardly any green. A patchwork of peat bogs. Some small hills. The east coast is rocky, with loads of inlets and channels and natural harbours. The west is totally different, with long white sandy beaches and dunes, exposed to the Atlantic gales and storm surges. Rare birds live here, like corncrakes and arctic terns. People come on holiday to see them. Less than one thousand people actually live on the island all year round.

Grandpa stopped at the brow of the hill to get his breath back. I stopped too.

He stared out to sea. 'You'd never know it,' he said. 'You never even get a glimpse. But they're out there all the same.'

'What are?'

'The islands of St Kilda,' Grandpa said. 'Dun, Soay, Boreray, Hirta.' He said their Gaelic names. 'Dùn, Sòthaigh, Boraraigh, Hiort.'

In the dim distance, I could make out the low shapes of the closer fishing islands, but nothing beyond. I thought of all the sea out there, going on and on towards St Kilda, deep and wild and dangerous.

I repeated the island names out loud. They sounded strange on my tongue. The words beat a rhythm in my head like a magic spell.

Dùn.

Sòthaigh,

Boraraigh,

Hiort.

Grandpa carried on down the hill.

I ran to catch up with him.

We got to my grandparents' house. It's a single-storey new-build, painted white, with big glass windows for the amazing view. Grown-ups go mad for views.

Granny waved from the open door, and I waved back.

'See you later, Jamie.' Grandpa turned up his track and I carried on to our house.

I went in the back door, into the kitchen. Mum was back already for lunch.

'Is that blood on your jeans?' she said. 'Did you cut yourself?'

'Not badly. I'm fine.'

Mum tutted. She shoved slices of cheese on toast under the grill. She turned to hug me and I ducked away.

I sniffed. 'You stink of fish,' I said.

She laughed. 'What's new? I've been sorting lobster and scallops all morning.'

Fee came into the kitchen. 'Disgusting. Fish? For lunch?'

'No, cheese on toast. And there's nothing disgusting about fish.'

Fee made a big show of laying the table. 'What have you done to your hand, Jamie?'

'Cut it, at the boat shed.' I showed her the wound.

'Disgusting. You should wash it. You'll get infected. And your hand will drop off.'

'You should,' Mum said. 'That looks sore, Jamie. Fee, no phones at the table.'

'It's important,' Fee said. 'Three new texts from Megan just pinged in. Because it's not raining there is an actual signal in this kitchen, for once.'

'Later.' Mum took the phone and put it on the dresser. 'Real life conversations only at mealtimes, Fee. You know that.'

Fee rolled her eyes.

I turned on the cold tap and ran water over my cut hand. It stung, and more fresh blood came out. I pressed a wad of towel on it to make it stop.

'Get Jamie a plaster, please,' Mum said to Fee.

Fee stomped off to the bathroom to find one.

Mum inspected my hand. 'Keep it clean and dry.' She kissed the top of my head before I had time to dodge away.

'Dad's back at the weekend,' Mum said. 'We should do something all together. Something fun.'

'Like what?' Fee was back.

'There's a ceilidh at the community hall, Saturday night. That would be fun.'

Fee sighed loudly. She peeled back the little paper bits on the plaster and made a big show of slapping it on my cut.

Mum looked annoyed but she didn't say anything. She grilled

second pieces of toast for me and her. Fee never has seconds. She eats less than a bird, Granny says.

Fee snatched back her phone as soon as Mum wasn't looking. I knew she was reading her messages under the table. I could have told Mum and dropped Fee in it, but I didn't. You never know when you might need a return favour from a big sister.

'I've got ten minutes for a cup of tea before I have to get back to work,' Mum said. 'What will you do this afternoon, Jamie?'

'Beach,' I said. 'And then boat shed again.'

'Good. Fee's going to help Granny, aren't you, darling?'

'Mmm. Yes.' Fee scrolled down her phone on her lap.

Mum didn't notice. She made tea in a pot and sat down again.

'Can we have a dog?' I said.

'Not that again,' Mum said. She looked at her watch. 'You two do the dishes, please. And hang the washing on the line to dry outside. It's a perfect day for it.'

Fee stuffed her phone in her pocket. She glared at me as if I'd said something. 'I'll do the washing up. You peg out the stuff.'

I piled the wet washing into the plastic basket and lugged it outside. Across the lochan, Granny's sheets and towels already flapped like flags. It's funny how the minute the sun comes out, everyone on the island hangs out washing. You have to use extra pegs because of the wind.

Way to the west, a car drove slowly along the causeway. It stopped halfway: for a family to watch a seal or an otter, perhaps. Most likely a seal. Otters are harder to spot, but there are lots, too, if you know where to look. There are road signs saying 'OTTERS CROSSING' even. The sun gleamed off the sea like sheet metal. The tide was coming in. I thought of the night when the high tide and a storm surge brought the sea right over the causeway and swept a car off it, and everyone inside the car drowned. They found the bodies washed up on the shore of the sea loch the next morning. I shuddered. I thought of Grandpa wanting me to learn to swim better.

Mum waved to me as she set off back to the Fisheries. Fee ran to catch her up. They walked together as far as Granny's. I could see for miles and miles over the water and the flat land—rough grass and bog, patches of white fluff from the bog cotton, peat stacked to dry, low white houses dotted along near the road. Rob and Euan would be helping their dads today. They cut the special meadow grass which grows on the sandy soil next to the sea—the machair—for hay in July and it takes all hands. Euan would be helping his dad with the sheep. Pavel was probably out on his dad's fishing boat. My dad was stuck in an office in the city. Poor Dad.

I kicked a ball over the white sand, dribbled it along the edge of the sea, dodged the waves looping up the beach. I kept going almost the whole length without getting wet.

And suddenly, there was the girl again—sitting on the rocks at the top of the beach, one hand on the dog. She must have been there all along, but I'd been concentrating on the ball, and the sea. In that second, when I looked up and saw her, a wave swished in and caught me.

She laughed at my wet legs. 'Should've rolled up your jeans.' She let go of the dog, and it ran towards me, tail wagging.

I crouched down to pat the dog. Its hair was wiry to touch; brown and grey. A terrier of some sort. Ears that folded down, whiskery eyebrows. A happy face.

'His name is Django,' the girl said. 'He wants your ball.'

I kicked the ball up the beach and the dog chased after it, but he didn't fetch it back. He tried to bite it but it was too slippery and big for him to grip with his teeth, so he lost interest. I jogged after the ball, dribbled it back.

The girl sat hunched up, her arms round her knees, as if she was cold. No wonder: she only had on a thin blue T-shirt with short sleeves, and a funny sort of skirt. Her hair was tied back with blue string, like something she'd picked up off the beach just now.

'What's your name?' she said.

'Jamie.'

'I'm Mara.'

'I saw you out in your boat this morning,' I said.

She turned sharply, as if she'd been caught out. Like I was spying on her. I explained. 'I was on the beach first thing. Your dog saw me. He barked.'

The dog, Django, sidled up as if he knew we were talking about him.

'What kind is he?' I asked her.

'Border terrier.' She ruffled the fur on his head. He had deep brown eyes; trusting eyes. Every time she stopped stroking him, he pawed her arm to make her start again.

'I'd like a dog,' I told her.

'You should get one,' she said. 'You've not long lived here, have you?'

'Three months.'

'I saw you move in. You live in the grey house with your sister and mum. You don't live with your dad, like me.'

'I do have a dad, but he has to work in Glasgow. He comes at weekends when he can.'

I'm nothing like you, I wanted to add.

What would my new friends say if they saw me talking to this strange girl, with her hippy clothes and matted hair?

'You don't go to our school,' I said. A simple statement; I didn't mean anything by it. But she whipped round, furious.

'I learn things other ways.' She spat the words.

I was sorry I'd upset her. I thought about what I could say next.

'Is it your boat?'

'Yes. *Stardust.*'

'You looked really good—you are really good at sailing, I mean.' The words came out wrong. But I could tell she was a bit pleased.

'I've had lots of practice. Been sailing since I was little.'

'Is it scary, out there by yourself?'

'No. Way too much to do to even think of being scared. I'll take you out, if you want. Your grandfather makes boats, doesn't he?'

'Yes. He's going to teach me.'

'Lucky. I'd love to do that.'

'I don't much like the sea. Being in it. Or on it.' There. I'd told her something I normally kept dead secret. How did *that* happen?

She didn't laugh. She didn't even seem shocked, or surprised.

She didn't say anything for a while.

'I can help you learn to sail, and to get used to the sea. To understand it. You don't have to like it.' She fiddled with the dog's collar. He lay in front of her, belly up, eyes closed. 'Plenty of sailors don't swim. They respect the sea too much.' She bent over Django, and he licked her face. 'Silly, gorgeous dog,' she said. She sounded softer now. Not prickly like before.

'Got to go.' I picked up the football. 'Helping my grandpa.' I walked on.

I looked back once. She was still sitting there, the dog at her feet. Her clothes—her hair—meant she fitted in with all the colours of the beach, like she was part of it: washed-out blue, gold, cream, her dark face a shadow.

I ran on.

The boat shed doors were wide open; I heard the shrill whine of the sanding machine. The air smelled of hot wood. Sawdust.

I knew something important had just happened, with that girl, but I didn't know what, exactly.

Mara's House

I kept seeing her, after that. Sailing in the sheltered bay, or skipping stones at the beach, or working the tideline, picking up driftwood and treasures. By accident I discovered where she lived: a strange, small shack at the top of a beach on one of the remote tidal inlets on the west side of the island.

I was cycling back from Rob's house—I'd been helping him and his brother stack peat in the shed next to their house—and I went along a rutted farm track on the edge of a field that wound round next to the sea, just to explore. See where it went. I was still finding my way around the island, discovering new places.

Far from any other houses, this small croft house was more like a shed than a home, but it had a garden and a gate, and stuff—driftwood, old fishing-net buoys, pebbles—arranged along the top of the wall. A wizened, windswept tree was hung with candle lanterns and strips of seaweed and bird feeders. I guessed straight away it was Mara's house. A bike was parked next to the wall, one of those old-fashioned bikes with a basket. A home-made trailer was hitched onto the back.

I didn't want Mara to think I was spying on her again. I turned back, towards the track near the sea. Something about how small the house looked, and how ramshackle, made me sad. I imagined how dark it would be inside with such tiny windows and the low roof. There were no neighbours near, nobody at all for a long way.

Perhaps Mara and her mum didn't have any friends. They seemed different from everyone else living here. Hiding away, like Grandpa said.

The track carried along next to the dunes, and then petered out. The sand was too deep to cycle through. I pushed the bike through a gap in the dunes, onto the beach itself.

The wind took my breath away. It came in gusts, whipped the loose dune sand into my face. A boat was scudding out in the bay, leaning into the wind. I recognized it—Mara's boat, with the dog on the bows. She seemed to be tugging down the mainsail;

the cloth flapped and billowed about her head, then tumbled down in a great bundle of canvas onto the deck as she let go of the rope. The dog barked and Mara waved and shouted something—she was too far out for me to hear what.

I ran closer. She was struggling to bring the boat in, the wind was so strong. The breaking waves close to the shore were swamping the boat. Before I could think about the danger, I kicked off my shoes and rolled up my jeans and waded in to help. I gasped. The water was freezing.

She threw the rope towards me, but it fell short. I took a deep breath, and waded deeper to catch hold of the rope, to help keep the boat more steady. She got the second sail down, and pulled up the centreboard. The dog jumped off and paddled to shore. I pulled on the rope, waded back to the beach, and the boat finally glided into the shallow water and she climbed out. I was shaking all over.

Mara laughed. 'That was fun!'

She was drenched, her hands red-raw with cold and salt. The boat was full of water.

It hadn't looked fun to me.

It had looked dangerous.

It *was* dangerous.

'Can you fetch the boat trailer?' Droplets of water flew from her hair as she moved, like when a wet dog shakes.

'Where from?'

'At the foot of the dunes, there.' She pointed.

I'd not noticed it, earlier. A rusty old trailer with two wheels, for pulling the boat. I pushed it down the beach for Mara and we lifted the dinghy onto the trailer. She was thin, and wiry, and stronger than she looked. We pulled the trailer up the beach, higher than the tideline, to keep it safe from the sea. She tied the boat rope around a big, flat stone to secure it.

Mara took off her life jacket and unzipped the top of her wet-suit. Underneath, she wore that same thin T-shirt, now soaked. She shivered. 'Come back for hot tea? My house is just up there.' She pointed.

I didn't tell her I already knew. Or that I didn't like tea. I followed her up the beach. I rolled down my wet jeans. My feet were blue with cold. I thought of how deep I'd waded in, to help her. What if I'd slipped?

My bike lay in the dunes where I'd abandoned it earlier.

'Yours?'

I nodded.

'Nice,' she said.

I wheeled it along the track next to her. Mara peeled her wet-suit down to her waist as we went along. She squeezed water out of her hair. Just looking at her made me cold all over again.

At the door, I hesitated. 'Will your mum be in?'

'Expect so. She's working. You'll be OK.'

I glanced behind, to check no one was watching. Who did I expect? Rob perhaps, or Euan. I didn't want them to know what I was doing.

Mara's mum was perched at a large wooden table under the window, a tray of paints spread out in front of her, next to a row of pebbles waiting to become seals and puffins. 'Hello,' she said, and carried on painting. So that was what Mara meant by *working*.

'I'll have a quick wash,' Mara said.

'Kettle's hot,' her mum said. I tried to remember the name Grandpa had told me. Ella? Emmy? Esme?

Mara took the kettle off the stove and carried it through to the bathroom. Weird.

'Sit.' Mara's mum pointed to an armchair covered with stuff.

Did she mean me? I put the pile of papers on the floor, and sat down. Django jumped up on my lap, all wet and smelly, but I let him stay. It was easier with him there. I stroked his wiry head. Bit by bit I relaxed. The wind rattled the windows and the room smelled of peat smoke, and it began to feel more cosy. Mara sang in the bathroom as she washed and changed, and her mother carried on dipping her brush into the paints, colouring her pebble creatures. I smoothed Django's head.

'How did you find us?' Mara's mum asked. 'I saw you outside, earlier. Did someone tell you the way?' Her voice sounded strange, kind of rusty, as if she wasn't used to talking much.

'No—by chance—' I stumbled over my words—'I was at the farm, at Paible. My friend lives there. And I came along the track by the dunes. Then I saw Mara in the boat.'

Mara reappeared. Her cheeks were pink and she was wearing a thick blue jumper and jeans, now. She refilled the kettle and put it on the stove.

Of course. No electricity. No hot water. No shower. Duh.

Her mother reached across the table and picked up a brown envelope from a pile of papers. 'There's another letter come.' She held it out to Mara. 'You'd better read it.'

'Not now,' Mara said quickly. 'Jamie's here for tea.'

'I should go, really,' I said.

'But you've only just come!'

I felt silly.

Mara's mother picked up her paintbrush. She muttered something under her breath.

'Pardon?' I said. I glanced at Mara.

'Nothing,' Mara said quickly. 'Take no notice.'

'Go! Go!' Mara's mum stared right at me. 'We didn't ask you here.'

'Stop it, Mam,' Mara said. '*I* invited Jamie. I'll make us hot chocolate. Now shush.'

All I wanted was to escape.

I watched Mara spoon hot chocolate powder from a tin into two mugs. We waited for a pan of water to heat up. No one spoke.

Mara's mum had a smear of white paint on her cheek and more on her lip, where she'd been sucking the brush. She went back to her painting.

She seemed different when she next spoke to me. More normal. 'You just moved here?'

'Three months ago.'

'You like it?'

'Yes. Much better than where we lived before. I even like school, here.'

Mara gave her mum a funny look.

'Only it's the holidays, now,' I said.

'How long do they give you?' Mara asked. 'How many weeks of *freedom* are you graciously allowed?'

'I'm not sure. Six, or seven, I think.'

Mara's mum picked up a piece of driftwood, studied the twisted shape. 'What do you reckon? Seahorse? Dragon?'

'Seahorse, definitely,' Mara said. She stroked the wood. 'Head here, this is the tail.'

All I saw was a bit of old wood.

Her mum began to draw on a pad of paper: a quick pencil sketch of a seahorse. It was good, but there was something strange about it, too: the scribbled lines, the way the pencil pressed too deep into the paper.

Mara and I sipped our hot chocolate. No one said anything. I was desperate to get out of there.

The dog jumped down from my lap and went to stand close to Mara. He whined. She patted his head.

I finished my drink. 'I'll go now.'

Mara nodded. 'I'll be sailing tomorrow morning. Want to come? Early, when the tide's high.'

'Thanks. I'm not sure . . . I'll have to see . . . '

'Be here by seven-thirty,' Mara said.

Did I want to sail? I thought about it as I cycled home. Would Mum allow me, anyway? Or should I not tell her?

The bike bumped along the rough track, back the way I'd come earlier. The road went between fields of machair, recently mown. The air was full of that sweet hay smell, and birdsong—skylarks and lapwings. The land was so flat and low, I could see for miles—small white houses dotted about—crofts, each with a small bit of land, and newer houses, built close to the road. Sheets and towels flapped on washing lines. People stacked peat, and raked hay on the fields. A few cars whizzed along the main road, making their way to the ferry, most likely.

It was a relief to be moving along, with all that space and the huge sky above. The wind battered and buffeted me, but it came from the sea, behind, and so it blew me fast towards home.

I imagined sailing on Mara's boat.

All that dark water, underneath. Going deep down, down, down. The wind and the tide pulling the boat out, out, out, away from the shore . . .

And then I remembered watching Mara sailing across the bay

in the bright sunshine; how exciting and free and wonderful it had looked.

Could I do that? Even if I was scared?

Could I?

The Boat

Did I dare? I lay awake that night as the wind gusted around the house. The sound of wild waves wove into my dreams when I did get to sleep, at last. It was midsummer, so it never got completely dark. I kept waking. I went to the window at five-thirty, and the sun was already well above the horizon, flooding the world with a shining, golden light. I opened the window wider; hardly any wind. Everything seemed possible on such a morning.

At six-thirty I got dressed quickly, quietly. I didn't have the right gear for sailing, so I shoved on shorts and a thick jumper, grabbed a waterproof jacket from the pegs in the hall, and shoved my feet into boots in the kitchen. I made a sandwich to take with me. Mum wouldn't mind me going out so early—it was the same most mornings. I left her a note on the table. Gone down to the beach. Back for lunch.

It was more or less true.

I got on my bike.

The dog barked as I came through the dunes. He raced up the beach to me. Mara was already getting the boat ready. She'd wheeled the trailer down the beach and was sorting out ropes and sails and stuff. She handed me a life jacket from a hatch at the back of the boat. 'Got a hat?'

I shook my head.

She rummaged again and produced a red woollen one.

I made a face.

'Put it on. You'll need it,' she said.

I stuffed it in my pocket.

She did everything on the boat so deftly and easily that I felt useless—I couldn't help with any of it, and how was I going to learn if she did it all so fast? But this first time wasn't a lesson; it was just a trip out in the bay, to show me what it was like.

'It's the perfect morning for a first sail. Light wind, small waves. You OK?'

'Yes.'

'So. We'll push her out deep enough to float her off the trailer, and get the centreboard down. You run back with the trailer, push it well up the beach, and I'll hold her till you get back. You'll get wet, mind. Take your boots off first.'

There wasn't a choice. Too late to back out now.

'It's freezing!' I waded out to the boat. It rocked in the breaking surf.

Mara was struggling to stop it sailing off completely; even without the big sail up, the wind and the tide were dragging the boat out to sea. The dog stood on the bows, tail wagging. He was used to this.

Waves washed in, drenching my shorts.

'Get on. Quick.' Mara hauled me on board, over the side. 'Sit there. Duck when the boom swings round, which it will when we gybe. Otherwise it could knock you out.'

'Unconscious?'

'No, overboard.' Mara laughed. 'Or maybe both.'

Did she guess how scared I was? I didn't tell her, but even that early on she seemed to know things without me saying a word.

She passed me a rope attached to the sail at the front. 'OK, you hold the sheet and fasten it to the cleat, there—that thing on the side—but be ready to slacken it off when I say. Keep the foresail smooth and flat; watch it the whole time.'

'And you steer?'

'You can have a go at the tiller later, if you like. Keep an eye on the water surface. Watch for a change on the face of the water when a squall comes—you'll see it before the wind catches the sail.'

Once we'd got out further, beyond the surf, the sea seemed to smooth out and it was a bit easier to balance. Django settled himself at my feet, his body warm against my leg.

'Where shall we go?' Mara shouted, above the creak of rope and sails and the rush of water under the bows.

'I don't know—not too far . . . ' I shouted back.

'Watch the horizon. That stops you getting sick. Look out!'

The boom swung round. I ducked just in time. The sail flapped and sagged as it lost the wind. The boat juddered, and swung round, and off we went again, scudding over the water. Spray broke over the boat. Everything was wet.

I turned my coat collar up, and fished in my pocket for the woollen hat.

'Told you!' Mara said.

I tried not to think about how deep the water was, beneath us. How far out we were. How sick I felt. I watched the horizon as if my life depended on it.

For a horrible moment I thought we were heading right out to sea, towards the uninhabited islands of Heisker and way beyond that, St Kilda. People used to sail to Heisker in the old days. Grandpa fished there when he was younger. The islands lay low in the water, as if they were whales, just surfacing. Grey shapes through the sea mist and spray. To get there you have to go through a line of rocks: the reef. Even this far away I could hear the churning surf pounding the rocks.

'Duck!' Mara yelled, and the boat turned again, heading south.

My heart steadied. Phew. We went parallel to the shore. The water smoothed out again. Django seemed to know where we were heading. He stood up, sniffed the air. He jumped onto the bows of the boat.

'I'll take you somewhere new,' Mara said. 'You won't have been to this bay. It's impossible to get here without a boat or a kayak. It's the best place to swim because it's sheltered from the wind.' She saw me flinch. 'It's OK, I know you don't want to. But I do.'

It was amazing, the way the wind dropped the moment we came round the south of the island. The sails flapped loose, the boat barely moved.

'How do we get closer?' I asked. There was no way I was going to swim from here.

Mara stood up and untied the ropes on the mainsail. The boat rocked with every movement. I held on to the side. Next she unstrapped two oars from under the wooden seat on the other side. I hadn't noticed them before. She pushed one over to me. 'Rest it in the special lock, on the edge—that keeps it in place.' She showed me how.

'Now shift over and sit in the middle of the boat, your back to the way we're going.' The boat rocked again as she moved next to me. 'Watch the angle of the oar as it hits the water. Don't dip too deep.'

She was good at it, of course, and I was rubbish, but I got better. It was hard to go straight, but I pulled harder, to match Mara's strength, and I got the rhythm almost right after a while, and we counted the strokes, *one, and one, and one . . .* and gradually we pulled nearer to the beach. Each time we lifted the oar, drops of water caught the sunlight, and glittered like crystals. It was mesmerizing; the rhythm of the oars, the light on the turquoise water, the rocking boat. Without the wind in the sail, it was quiet, magical. We stopped counting aloud. For the first time, I began to enjoy being on the boat.

The next time I looked over my shoulder, I saw the beach properly: a perfect round cove, totally sheltered from the wind, with the whitest sand, and a dune cliff behind. A small blue rowing boat was anchored close to the beach, half stranded by the dropping tide.

'Stow your oar and get the foresail down, Jamie. Quick.'

My hands were clumsy as I unwound the rope. The sail tumbled down in an awkward clutter of cloth. I tried to smooth it and fold it neat.

'What will we do with the boat?'

'Anchor her out here and wade in.' Already, she was lowering the long anchor chain. She did everything so easily, gracefully, as if she was part of it; part of the boat, the sea, the chain . . . I know that sounds weird, but it's the truth.

The waves washed in gently, trickled with light. Everything shone and glittered. The sun was warm on my back. I could *almost* imagine swimming.

I ran along the beach to warm up. Mara searched slowly along the high tideline for stuff washed up. Django ran between us, chasing after the seabirds when they landed close.

I jogged back to see what Mara had found. She held out her hand to show me her collection of shells and the seeds she called sea beans, all the way from the Caribbean.

'The island is a good place, 'cause of the currents. The Gulf Stream brings warmer water up here and washes stuff up.' She showed me mermaids' purses, which are the egg cases of dogfish, and chalky white cuttlefish bones, light as air. 'These are my favourite shells of all.' She trickled some into my palm. 'Go on, look really closely.'

The shells were tiny, translucent pink and white, lemon-shaped with tiny ridges on the top and an opening on the smooth underside like a mouth.

'Aren't they lovely?' Mara said. '*Trivia arctica*: northern cowrie. Marine gastropod mollusc. Stone-age people made them into jewellery. And cowries were used as money in lots of places, once upon a time.'

We went along the tideline, searching for more. We filled our pockets.

Mara stopped to check the tide. 'We'll get stuck here, if the tide goes out too far. Got to keep an eye out.' She pulled off her jumper. 'I'm going to swim. You?'

I shook my head. I ran further along the beach. Django ran with me.

I let myself pretend he was my dog. I threw him a stick but he only went after it half-heartedly. I called his name, and he raced back to me. 'Good dog,' I said. He looked at me, and he put his tongue out a little way and licked the air.

'Good boy, Django.' I stroked his ears: velvet-soft, not like his wiry body.

He raced away again. He barked at the terns diving at us as we went too close to their nesting places. I kicked a plastic bottle along and Django joined in, chasing and playing as if it were a proper ball.

When I next looked back, Mara was swimming across the bay, a tiny head bobbing above the water. If it had been me, I'd have been worried about the cold, about poisonous jellyfish, about currents sweeping me out of my depth. She was afraid of nothing. She was completely herself.

I wished I could be more like her.

Not *like* her, exactly. More, able to be *my*self, the way she was *her*self.

Django trotted ahead. He stopped to look back at me, and off he bounded again. His tail was high, his ears flapped.

I watched Mara: a tiny dot in the middle of all that blue. I shivered. What would I do if something happened to her—a shark, or something like that, or if she got swept out? You can get cramp, swimming in cold sea . . .

Django barked and barked. What had he found? He was jumping and barking like crazy.

'It's OK, I'm coming!' I yelled.

He'd gone way ahead while I was watching Mara.

I got closer. There was a disgusting smell. He'd found something dead and rotting. He was rolling in it. Yuck. 'Oi, Django, Stop that!' I called.

He tugged at the dark mound of stinking flesh.

I gagged. Whatever it was had died a while ago. It was rotten and revolting, buzzing with flies and crawling with maggots. Sea gulls or something had pecked out the eyes and torn off chunks of the bloated body.

Not a fish, something much bigger.

A dolphin, perhaps, or a porpoise.

I pulled Django away and dragged him back along the sand with me. He didn't like it. He whined and dug his feet in and yelped.

The beach didn't seem so perfect any more. I couldn't get rid of the smell. It followed me, as if the air itself was infected. Duh! The dog had rolled in the rotten pulpy flesh, hadn't he? The smell was on his fur.

I dragged him by his collar down to the sea and pushed him deeper, so he had to swim. He hated me for that. He wriggled free and ran back to the beach, shaking his fur, a smaller, flatter, skinnier version of himself now he was soaked to the skin. But he still stank. I could smell it from where I was, it was that strong. I went to grab him again. He growled.

Mara must have been watching. I suddenly heard her yelling my name.

'What are you DOING?' She was wading to the shore, waving her arms and yelling at me.

I let go of the dog. He sprinted towards her, shaking his fur as he went, like a cartoon dog.

I waded along through the shallow water. My legs were numb to the cold by now.

Django was going mad, jumping and whining and making high-pitched little shrieks, wagging his tail with relief or joy or something. She picked him up and held him tight.

'He rolled in a dead dolphin!' I called. 'He stinks. I was only trying to wash it off.'

Mara glared at me. She turned and walked away, the dog still in her arms.

She kept walking, her back to me.

Typical. Now she was in a mood with me. And for what?

Huh. I turned my back, and went the other way.

I searched for cowrie shells further along the beach but I didn't find any. The shells here were those white limpet ones, and navy blue mussels, but all crushed into bits, as if they'd been turned and smashed by a wilder sea.

I kept walking. The beach was wider here, a huge expanse of wave-ridged wet sand dotted with pebbles and lumps of green weed, crossed by channels of water like shallow river deltas. Everything was bright, beautiful, shining in the sunlight. I thought about damming one of the channels, diverting the streams to make a bigger pool . . . and then I realized. The beach was this massive because the tide had gone way, way out.

I remembered what Mara had said earlier. How we mustn't leave it too long, or we'd be stuck here.

I looked back. I must have come round the headland without realizing. I couldn't see Mara any more.

The sea was different here. It was darker, deeper, a churning current as it swept round the headland. It made my chest go tight, seeing how strong it was. I imagined losing my balance, slipping on the sandy edge, and going down deep. I shuddered. I ran back the way I'd come, my heart banging in my chest.

As I came round the headland I could make out a tiny figure, way out. Mara was wading out to the boat. She had the dog in her arms. She didn't turn round, didn't seem to hear, even when I ran along the edge of the sea and yelled and waved my arms. She climbed into the boat. I heard the rattle of the anchor chain as she pulled it up. The dog barked from the bows, but the boat was already drifting out, and by then she must have got the oars locked in, because she began to row, and the boat moved steadily, purposefully out to sea. She refused to look in my direction. It was as if I didn't exist, as if she'd forgotten all about me. I'd dropped out of her world completely.

Stranded

Surely she wouldn't just leave me here?

Or maybe she would.

Her moods changed as quickly as the island sky.

I sat on the sand and watched the boat get smaller and further way. I saw her raise the sails. I kept expecting her to change direction, to come sailing back into the bay, laughing and saying it was all a joke. But the boat disappeared around the headland. She had sailed off and left me behind.

I sat for ages, still not quite believing what had happened. A weird kind of quiet settled over everything. The waves washed in, birds dived and swooped, wind blew through the dunes and rattled the dry grass. And I sat and stared at the empty sea. What now?

I wandered over to the small rowing boat. It lay on its side, stranded a very long way from the sea. Whoever it belonged to had removed the oars. Not that there would have been the remotest chance of me rowing myself back. The thought of being out there alone on the deep water . . . the tide dragging the boat out to sea . . .

I explored the beach. I found a kind of animal track winding up the cliff. It was a cliff made of sand: massive steep sand dunes, bound together by sharp-edged marram grass. I kept slipping back, but I scrabbled my way up and finally got to the top.

I stood on the ridge and looked over. The other side seemed to be nothing but bog, ridges of rough grass criss-crossed by shiny channels of water reflecting sky.

A bird with a curved beak took off from one of the pools. Curlew. Its ghost cry echoed over the watery land. There was no sign of anyone.

I turned to face the way I'd come. The tide had gone far out, leaving a huge expanse of ridged wet sand. But someone would come back for that rowing boat, eventually. Wouldn't they? Maybe they would rescue me.

I slithered back down the dune hill. I was hungry. My breakfast sandwich already seemed a long time ago.

I imagined I was Robinson Crusoe on my own island. I dammed the stream and diverted the channels. I collected more shells. I gathered driftwood for a fire, and then realized I had no matches or anything to light it.

No one came back to the rowing boat.

The tide turned. I scanned the sea for signs of other boats, but nothing came. I played Hit the Can with pebbles and a broken plastic bottle. I found a tiny crab living inside a shell. The seabirds screamed and dived at me when I got too close.

Still nothing. No boats, no planes; nothing but seabirds and sandflies. I was hungry and thirsty.

I remembered a news story about three men whose boat capsized in the Pacific ocean. They swam to a deserted island. They made the word HELP out of pebbles, in huge letters on the sand. They were spotted by an American Navy airplane and rescued. I wrote big letters in the sand with a stick of driftwood. **HELP! STRANDED!** I imagined the air-sea rescue helicopter flying over and seeing me . . . winching me up . . . the helicopter pilot talking on his radio . . . Mum driving to meet me off the plane at the airfield on Benbecula . . . Telling the story to Rob and Euan, later.

The sky stayed empty and blue and silent.

The tide crept in, slowly at first, but then something changed, and it speeded up, the waves flooding up the beach. The strip of sand got smaller. How high would the sea come? Eventually it reached the rowing boat, lapped around it, lifted and floated it in on its mooring.

What if the sea came right up the beach? I scrambled back up the dunes. There had to be a way back across the marsh.

Where before had been channels of water between boggy strips of reed grass was now a sheet of water gleaming like polished metal in the sunlight. There was no dry land left at all. This must be tidal salt marsh. At high tide it was completely flooded.

I was stuck.

It must be way later than lunchtime. Mum would be panicking. She'd have found out from Grandpa that I hadn't shown up at the boat shed all morning. She'd have searched the nearest beaches.

I scanned the horizon for the sign of a boat.

Nothing but sea, and rocks, and the roar of the surf breaking over the reefs out towards the fishing islands, even louder now. Directly below me, the sea had washed out the letters in the sand. My pile of driftwood for a fire was floating, returned to flotsam. The rowing boat bobbed and tugged at its mooring as if it might break free at any moment.

So stupid, to have gone out in Mara's boat in the first place. To think she'd behave like a normal person. Why had I been such an idiot?

Euan and Rob would find out. Everyone at school would laugh. Mum would go mad. She'd stop me going out for the rest of the summer.

I curled up in a hollow in the sand dunes.

Time seemed to slow down totally. Nothing changed.

Spears of dry marram grass rattled in the wind.

Maybe I'd be there forever. Years later someone would find my curled up body, a dried-out husk, the shell of a boy, and make up a story of what had happened there.

Sail

I opened my eyes. Above me, blue sky; a fringe of pale gold dune grass. For a second I didn't have the foggiest idea where I was. I'd been dreaming, there'd been a noise—or was that still part of the dream? I'd been lost, people calling my name, a dog barked . . .

A V of geese tracked steadily overhead, honking.

Wind in the dry grass. A curlew's cry.

The honking sound got fainter, the line of geese disappeared into the blue.

My face burned from too much wind and sun.

The tide must surely have gone down by now. I scrambled up to get a better view. For a second I went dizzy and the world span.

Out to sea: a smudge of something.

I blinked, to be sure.

A flash of sunlight. Something white.

Surf breaking over rock?

Or the wash of a boat?

A sail?

It was very far off. Tiny.

A boat?

Impossible to tell which way it was going, if it was.

My eyes watered with staring so hard. But I began to hope.

It was nearer, now. Definitely a boat. Two white sails.

A small dinghy tacked back and forth out in the bay, getting closer with each turn.

I waved wildly. I slid and skidded down the dunes towards the sea and stood in the shallow water.

A dog barked. I saw the small figure at the back.

Gradually, the boat came close enough for me to be sure it was Mara.

I waded out and grabbed on to the edge of the boat.

Django raced to the bows and wagged his tail.

Mara reached out to heave me over the side.

I tumbled ungracefully into the boat. It rocked, and I steadied myself and clambered onto the seat. I put on the wet life jacket she handed me. Water dripped off me onto the deck. I shook with cold.

'You came back!' I blurted out.

She laughed. 'Of course I came back, soon as the tide was right. Don't be daft.'

'But why did you go off like that, in a huff?' I asked. 'What did I do?'

She didn't answer. She fished under the seat for a plastic bag and shoved it at me. She grabbed the tiller and steered the boat to meet a big wave as it rolled in.

'Bread. And a hard-boiled egg if you want. And cake.'

I guess that was her way of saying sorry.

I ate everything in massive hungry gulps.

Django sat at my feet, drooling.

'Was it wonderful, having the beach all to yourself?' Mara said.

I stared at her.

'Did you have a great time in paradise?'

She was serious. It *was* her idea of heaven.

'No,' I said.

She gave me a look, as if maybe I wasn't the person she'd hoped I was.

'What time is it?' I said.

'I have no idea.'

'Mum will be worried about me,' I said. 'I've been here for hours and hours.'

'But why would she worry?'

'Of course she'd worry!' I said. 'Any mum would.'

Mara sighed. 'OK. We'll go back. This time, you will have a go at the tiller.' She wasn't giving me a choice.

We swapped seats. She showed me what to do. She was a good teacher. She stayed calm. She didn't shout. She laughed a lot.

I stopped worrying so much about making a mistake. I laughed and laughed when the boom swung round and nearly knocked her flying.

We'd come round the headland. We had to tack, to keep the wind in the sail. Tacking is when the boat zigzags. Each time you turn, the boom swings round and you have to duck and adjust the sails and everything happens in a rush.

Already I could see Mara's beach, where we'd sailed from all those hours ago. Any minute now we'd turn into the bay.

Further out to sea was that line of breaking surf. Choppy water.

'If we kept sailing west, we'd eventually get to the fishing islands,' Mara said. 'If we could get through the reef, that is. And if we kept on going, we could sail all the way to St Kilda.'

'No way! It's much too dangerous!'

I thought of those tiny remote islands—Dun, Soay, Boreray and Hirta—way out in the Atlantic ocean, right at the edge of the world. A long time ago people lived their entire lives there. Not now.

Colonies of gannets endlessly circle the thousand-foot cliffs, dark against the sky. Boat trips go there, sometimes, in summer when it isn't too rough. Boats with engines, and life jackets, and safety equipment, and even then they often have to turn back. The sea is treacherous.

'We won't sail there today.' Mara smiled. She edged over and took the tiller from me.

The boat turned and the wind dropped out of the sail.

'One day I will,' Mara said. She stared dreamily out to sea, to where the St Kilda islands must be—too far out for us to see them. 'Imagine sailing there. Living in one of the stone houses . . . being self-sufficient, like the old islanders.'

I shivered. 'You'd probably die.'

Mara frowned. 'Are you scared of *everything*, Jamie? Don't you dream of adventures, too?'

I didn't answer. I kept my eyes firmly on the land ahead.

'You get ready to jump out and fetch the trailer.'

She guided the boat through the breaking waves and into shallow water.

I jumped off and waded to shore. Django came with me. I was shivering, soaked to the skin. But my feet were on land that kept still, instead of a boat deck dipping and turning and rocking under me. I staggered up the beach, giddy with the relief of it.

I dragged the trailer down to the boat, and helped Mara get it out of the water. My arms ached, my head ached with too much sun and wind, but I knew something had changed.

I thought about it as I cycled home.

I had this new feeling inside me. New, and strange, and wonderful.

I had actually sailed a boat. Even though I'd been terrified at first, I had sailed Mara's boat.

By myself.

Out at sea.

Grandpa would be dead proud of me.

Not that I could ever tell him, of course. He'd go ballistic if he found out what I'd just done.

Now I had to work out what on earth to tell Mum.

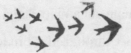

I threw down the bike on the grass near the back door. There was no sign of Mum's car. What did that mean? I pulled off my boots in the porch. Took a deep breath.

Fee was in the kitchen.

'Where's Mum?'

'Work, of course. Till 5, like always.'

She gave me a weird look. 'Stop panicking. I told her you were at Rob's at lunchtime. I lied for you, Jamie Mackinnon. So you'd better be eternally grateful.'

'I am,' I said. I really was.

'So where were you? And why are your clothes soaked and what's happened to your face?'

'My face?'

'And your head, duh-brain. Go look in the mirror.'

A day in the sun and wind had turned my face scarlet. And my arms and my legs. When I peeled off my wet things in the bathroom, I looked ridiculous. White torso, red everything else.

So it was the sunburn that Mum got cross about, when she did come home after work. I didn't have to say anything else. She went on and on and on about the dangers of sunstroke and skin damage. She made me promise to put sun cream on in future. She slathered me in lotion to soothe the burn.

It could have been so much worse.

Later, while she got supper ready, she told Fee and me about a Polish girl called Pia who had come to work at the Fish Processing Factory for the summer. 'She's lovely,' Mum said. 'A breath of fresh air.'

'Why on earth would she want to come here to work?' Fee said. 'Nothing happens. There's nothing to do. Nowhere to go. And what summer, exactly?'

'Today was beautiful,' Mum said. 'We've had two sunny days in a row! As Jamie will vouch for.' She ruffled my hair and I let her, for once. Best to keep my mouth shut.

I spread out Mum's big-scale paper map of the island on the kitchen table. The place names on the map were written in Gaelic and most of it was coloured in blue: water. I couldn't find the deserted beach. I searched for St Kilda too, but that was too far, way off the edge of the map.

'Clear the map away now, Jamie,' Mum said. 'Dinner's nearly ready.'

The house phone rang. Fee rushed to answer it. I heard her chatting to Dad, begging him to let her come and live with him in Glasgow. 'It's the pits,' she said. 'I will die of boredom if you make me stay here.'

Mum and I looked at each other. 'She'll get over herself,' Mum said. 'She can't help being a teenager.' She laughed. 'Hope you don't get like that.'

'I won't,' I said. 'Not ever.'

'Promise?'

I nodded. I bundled up the map.

'Fold it properly!' Mum said. She went to talk to Dad in the hall. She told him about the community ceilidh at the weekend. Said the weather was really good. Work was fine, there was a new girl . . .

I stopped listening.

Dad hadn't been back to us for nearly three weeks. It was weird, how we'd got used to it. At first we'd missed him like mad. But I didn't like talking on the phone. I couldn't think of what to say. Skype was even worse. The island internet connection was rubbish.

When Dad was actually here, we didn't have to talk; we could do stuff together, which was the whole point.

Fee put her head round my door, later. 'So, little brother, where were you all day? With your girlfriend? I've seen you with that weird kid on the beach.'

'Shut up and go away!' I kicked the door shut in her face. She was horrible, my sister. I hoped she wouldn't say anything to Mum.

Ceilidh Dance

Dad arrived on the Saturday early evening, just in time for family supper. Fish, of course. Scallops fried in garlic and butter and chilli, the way Dad likes them. The ceilidh was in full swing by the time we turned up.

One dance finished and straight away people got ready for the next. 'Everyone make a circle,' the caller shouted. 'Join hands.'

The music picked up pace. Mum grabbed Dad's arm and pushed him into the circle with her.

'Into the middle and clap.'

'Free drinks over there.' Fee's new friend Suze steered her over to the table. Fee and Suze would be going together to the big school on the south island when school started up again after the holidays.

Dad mouthed something at Fee as he danced past but she took no notice.

The table was stacked with bottles of booze; you could help yourself and no one checked how old you were or how much you drank. I watched Suze pour whisky into two plastic cups as if it was orange juice.

The music speeded up. The dancers swung round in pairs, wild with laughter.

Through the open door at the back of the community centre I spotted Rob and Euan outside on the wall. I dodged past the dancers and went out to join them.

Euan passed me a can of fizzy drink.

'Blimey,' I said. 'It's crazy in there.'

Rob shoved me. 'Can't keep up the pace?'

I shoved him back.

He pretended to fall off the wall backwards, only he was still holding on, and he hauled himself back up and pulled a clown face as he reappeared.

Two girls from school were watching. They smiled. Rob did his trick again. The girls turned away, like they'd had enough of us fooling around. They went back inside. The three of us sat on the wall. The air was heavy with damp. We kicked the wall and didn't speak. We picked up stones and aimed at an empty can on the bog the other side of the wall. Rob won three rounds out of five.

Dad came to the open door. He beckoned me over. 'Come on, Jamie. Your mum says you have to dance this one with your sister. We're short of men.'

Euan grinned. He pulled Rob with him. 'You'll be needing us, then,' he told my dad.

Everyone on the island knows all the dances; they learn them from when they're little, and the boys dance as well as the girls. It's not like it was back at my city school, where no one would be seen dead dancing like this. Or holding a girl's hand, for that matter.

People took their places; sets of eight: four couples in each. My dad and mum were partners, of course. When Dad finally gets here Mum wants to keep him really close. He kept snatching kisses and made her laugh when he swung her round so fast her feet left the ground.

My sister grabbed me. 'Shut up,' she said, before I'd even opened my mouth. 'Don't speak. Dance, idiot boy.'

Euan and Rob each stood next to one of the girls who'd been watching us earlier.

The dance started easy. Two lines, into the middle, clap, and back. Repeat. Then the men peeled off in a line one way and the girls the other, and as they got round to the bottom the first couple made an arch and we all went through, and then you swung your partner around and got dizzy. Or something like that. On to the next bit: weaving and swinging and spinning . . . The dance got more complicated as the fiddle and accordion speeded up.

I tried to copy the others, but I hadn't got a clue what to do, really.

Fee got crosser and crosser with me. 'WATCH my feet, you goon.' Finally she flounced off in an enormous strop, just when it was our turn to make the arch.

Mum and Dad tutted. Fee disappeared outside.

A dark-haired girl stepped up and took Fee's place. She took my hands and wc made the arch. The dance carried on, couples stepped through our arch. I knew Wren from school: she was in the year below us. Good at running and dancing and science. She grabbed my hands and swung me round, laughing all the while. We swung, faster and out of control, half-falling in our giddiness.

A group of older ladies sat at one of the tables, chatting together. I heard fragments of their conversation as Wren and I swung close. I heard them say Mara's name.

—It's more than bad for Mara. It's downright wrong . . .

I wondered what they meant. What was wrong? But the dance whirled on, there was no time to listen to any more, and I forgot all about it.

I had a good time, better than I'd expected, better than my sister Fee, out on the wall, drinking something that made her sick in the car on the way home, later, and our dad furious.

There was a huge row when we got home. I left them to it. Climbed into bed, still hot and sweaty from the dancing. Dad was back, and we were a family again. And it was Fee in trouble, not me.

I didn't see Mara for a while. With Dad there, we were busy with family stuff. He took me fishing. We didn't catch anything and I got bitten by midges, which itched and itched, and I scratched the bites till they were red and sore and Mum slathered calamine lotion on my arms and legs. Mum and Dad had long talks at the kitchen table about jobs, and money, and how it would be if Dad could get work on the island. Fee went to stay over at Suze's house for a night.

Dad went back on the ferry on Tuesday. We waved goodbye at the harbour terminal. Mum turned away so we wouldn't see she was crying, but we saw anyway. Fee was actually nice to me all the way home.

On Wednesday, it was back to normal, and I was supposed to be helping Grandpa at the boat shed.

I got my bike out. It was drizzling. Instead of going along the beach, I cycled along the single-track road. A white van came whizzing up behind me, and I stopped to let it go past.

What made me look up? Possibly the flash of movement, or the light catching the white page of what I took to be a book, but turned out not to be. Mara was perched on the hill above the shore road. I turned the bike round and cycled towards the hill instead of going along the shore to the boat shed. I left my bike at the road edge, wheels still spinning, and scrambled up the tufty grass to the top.

Mara was staring at a page of typed writing: a letter. Django lay beside her. He wagged his tail when he saw me.

I flopped down beside them on the damp grass.

Mara stuffed the letter into her bag. She had her head down so her hair hid her face. For a second I thought she was crying. But she straightened up, and twisted her hair into a plait over one shoulder, and she seemed fine.

'Hello, Jamie,' she said. 'Welcome to Compass Hill.'

'Why Compass Hill?' I asked. ''Cause it's round? Or something to do with directions?' I was out of breath. The hill wasn't high, but it was steep.

'I don't know. Maybe it was a landmark for sailors coming home from the off-islands,' Mara said. 'Helped them find the gap through the reefs, and a safe passage. On a clear day when the light is right, you can see from here all the way to St Kilda. There's a viewing point further up the road, with a telescope for tourists to look through.'

We both stared out to sea. Low cloud and mist blurred the line between sea and sky. You could hardly see any distance today. Not the fishing islands, not anything. The drizzle turned to proper rain.

Django whined.

'He's bored, Mara said.' And he really doesn't like getting wet.'

'Who does?'

'The gulls don't mind it. Or the curlews and terns, the

sandpipers and oystercatchers.' She passed me the binoculars she had round her neck.

I wiped the glass on my jumper hem.

On the beach far below small brown birds scurried along the edge of the sea.

Beads of damp had settled on Mara's coat, her hair, her eye-lashes.

'Where are you heading, anyway?' Mara said.

'The boat shed.'

Mara looked at me.

'The long way round,' I added.

She smiled. 'The extremely ridiculously long way round.'

I didn't tell her that I'd changed direction when I saw her on the hill.

'Can I come?' Mara asked.

I nodded.

'Will your granddad mind?'

'Grandpa. No. You can help.'

She pulled her hood up. 'Come on, then.'

We slipped and slithered down the wet grass to the road. I pushed the bike; we walked together. Django trotted beside us, his tail half mast.

'All right, Django?' I patted his damp fur. He looked up at me like he was smiling. Dogs definitely can smile, in their own doggy way. One day, I'd have a dog of my own.

The boat shed was warm and dry. We took off our wet coats and hung them on the hooks by the door. If Grandpa was surprised to see Mara he didn't let on.

Marek was working in the shed with Grandpa today, painting an old wooden boat that had come in for repairs.

'Do you know Pia, the new girl at the Fisheries?' I asked Marek. 'She's from Poland too.'

He shook his head. His face was red. Maybe because Mara was there. Marek's shy. He never says much.

Grandpa came over.

Mara piped up. 'I'd like to watch you and learn how to build a clinker boat, please.'

Grandpa smiled. He hadn't expected that. He nodded at her.

'Can I help Marek with painting the other boat?' I said.

Grandpa nodded. 'We're up against the clock with the re-fit. Watch how Marek holds the brush, and don't take on too much all at once. Hold it steady and even. Go gently with the grain of the wood, all in one direction. There's a knack to it.' Grandpa pointed to the overalls hanging on a nail. 'Best put those on first. Your mum won't be happy if you come home covered in paint.'

Mara pulled over a stool and watched as Grandpa fitted the wooden ribs into the hull of the new build. From time to time she asked a question, and he answered it. They got along fine. Django slept at her feet, his head on his paws. Marek and I painted the hull of the old boat in the shed, in for repairs. The paint wasn't like ordinary house paint; it was gloopy and smelled of tar. It was a deep blue, the colour the sea goes as evening falls.

Marek and I both listened to Mara, chatting away. She asked Grandpa about the old days when he sailed and fished.

'What's it like, going through the reef?'

'Dangerous. You have to pick the weather and the right state of the tide,' Grandpa said. 'It's all a question of timing, and good judgment. You get a feel for it with practice. You know by the sound of the surf. When it's really pounding, you don't even try. And you need to know your boat. What she can handle. Get it wrong and you will die.'

Mara listened carefully and nodded. She was like a sponge, soaking in knowledge.

'And what if you get through one way, but can't get back?'

'There's stone huts on the fishing isles,' Grandpa said. 'You take provisions. Make a fire with driftwood. You've got the fish, and gulls' eggs if need be. You can ride out a storm over several days, as long as you get the boat into shelter. There's a natural harbour on the east side of the nearest island. In the old days, whole families lived out there.'

'So what kind of boat is best?'

'The traditional ones, of course, that we build here. *Never broken in a sea*, that's what we say. And it's the truth.'

Mara was quiet for a while.

'So, a small dinghy like mine . . . ?'

'Well, she's a tough little boat, and you can handle her well. I've seen you out in the bay in a squall. But don't try to get through the reef by yourself, lass. It's too dangerous. Your mother would not be happy about that, now, would she?'

Mara shrugged. I guess she knew her mother much better than Grandpa did.

Grandpa carried on working. I was surprised that he was happy to chat to Mara while he worked. She sat still and watched his every move, Django sleeping at her feet. Marek and I painted the other boat. Rain drummed on the tin roof but we didn't mind, safe and dry inside. We worked till lunchtime.

After that, Mara came with me to the boat shed most mornings. She watched and listened carefully. She wanted to try everything. Grandpa gave her little jobs to do, and she learned how to use the saw and chisel and plane much quicker than I did. She asked questions all the time. She wanted to know if Grandpa had ever sailed to St Kilda. She wanted to know what it was like on the island with the stone houses where people had lived out their lives at the edge of the world.

'I've never been there,' he told her. 'It's a long and tricky sail. We rarely get the weather for it. But I've a book about the place, if you want to see some photos. I'll bring it here if you want.'

He brought it the next day. She pored over those pictures. She looked at them every time she came to the shed. Like they held something special and secret that she longed for.

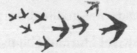

It was about a week later, a Thursday. A rare sunny morning, after a week of rain, and I wanted to stay longer on the beach. But Mara was keen to get to the boat shed, and I couldn't let her go and see my grandpa on her own. I didn't want her listening to his stories about the old days and the islands without me.

Maybe Mara was like the daughter he'd wanted my mum to be: interested in everything to do with boats and the sea, happy and hard-working.

'You're a natural,' Grandpa told Mara, that Thursday afternoon. 'You've a good eye. Your hands have the language.'

How can hands have language?

Mara nodded as if she understood him perfectly.

'I had high hopes that my Kathleen would take to it like that,' Grandpa said. 'But she never had any interest in the boats. She was all for getting away, going to the mainland, like so many of the young people these days. And then when she got there, she was miserable.'

'Why did she stay living there so long, then?' I butted in.

'Because she met your dad. Fell in love. And the city was where his work was. And you kids came along, and that was that.'

'Till now!' Mara said. She grabbed my arm and swung me around. 'Now you're here! Hurrah! Happy ever after.' She ran out of the shed into the sunshine.

Grandpa laughed. 'She's a happy soul today. She's a lovely lass, your friend. But she's a tricky one, too, Jamie. Take care.'

I took no notice of his warning. I ran after Mara. Her happiness was catching. I wanted to run and run along the beach, run up to Compass Hill, go out in the boat. I wanted it all.

I followed her along the single-track road past the freshwater lochan. There were ducks swimming on it. Two geese took off as we got close.

'Look!' Mara said. 'One tiny duckling's been left behind!' We stopped to watch. The smallest duckling was still on the bank, scared to jump in after its brothers and sisters, and the mother duck hadn't noticed.

Peep peep peep. The duckling called plaintively from the bank.

'Hold Django for me,' Mara said.

I took his collar and made him sit.

Mara slid down the steep bank towards the lochan. The duckling panicked. It plopped in. The lake water was so clear we could see its tiny webbed feet paddling like mad. Mara laughed. 'We should teach you to swim here, Jamie.'

'I *can* swim,' I said. 'I just don't like it much.'

'If you got better and stronger at it you might like it more.'

Mara took off her trainers and dangled her feet in the peaty water. 'It's warm!' she said. 'Try it.'

I slid down the bank next to her. I leaned down and tested the water with my hand. 'Not warm,' I said. 'Cold. Wet.'

Mara laughed. 'Chicken,' she said. 'It's much warmer than the sea.'

'How deep is it?' I peered into the water. The peat at the bottom of the loch turned it gold, like whisky.

'Shallow at the edge, deadly deep in the middle.' Mara smiled at me. 'I've got a good idea. You can practise swimming here. Go and get your swimming things and we'll start today.'

'No way,' I said. It was all right at the edge, maybe, where I could see the bottom. But not further out. I knew Mara was teasing me, but *deadly deep* might be the truth of it.

Django whined at us from higher up the bank. We were making him nervous.

'Think about it.' She corrected herself. 'No, don't think about it, just get on with it. Go home and get your swimming stuff. I'll meet you back here.'

She scrambled back to her dog. He wagged his tail and barked and they ran on together. She didn't wait for me. She didn't say goodbye, either. I was used to that now.

The Lochan

It was quarter to six. Was I going or not? I had my swimming shorts on under my jeans, just in case. She'd already be there with Django by now. It wasn't fair to let her down, was it? And the water was shallow at the edge, you could easily stand up. Except, there was no telling how quickly it got deep. There might be fish with teeth and blood-sucking bugs like leeches . . .

'What's the matter with you?' Fee asked. 'Got ants in your pants? You're making the table rock, the way you're jigging about.' She sawed a hefty slice of bread and shoved it in the toaster. 'How many slices?'

'Eh? What?'

'How many slices of toast? I'm making your tea, duh-brain.'

'Oh, but I'm going out.' I'd made the decision. I grabbed a towel from a pile of laundry in the porch as I went past, shoved it in my backpack, and ran out of the back door.

I wished I'd brought my bike. It seemed further, going this way. I stopped to get my breath. In the distance seabirds cried and the sea crashed and pounded on the rocks. High tide.

A truck bumped along the road some way behind me. I turned round. It looked familiar. It slowed down as it got close. Yes. Thought so. Rob's dad's truck.

Rob wound down the window. 'Where're you going, Jamie?'

'Nowhere,' I lied. I thought fast. No way could I mention Mara. Swimming with her. Anything like that.

'OK. Hop in,' Rob's dad said. 'And we'll take you nowhere.' He laughed.

'Football at ours?' Rob said. 'Euan's coming over.'

I nodded, and climbed in the front with them.

I slid down in the seat as we got closer to the loch, in case Mara was already waiting and saw me.

I glanced back through the rear window once we we'd gone past. Yes, there she was, paddling at the edge of the lochan in a faded blue swimsuit, with her skinny brown legs and arms. Django sat on the bank next to her towel, watching her.

'Mad as a snake, that girl,' Rob said. 'What does she think she's doing in the loch? Weird.'

'Like mother like daughter,' Rob's dad said. 'But I guess they've had a hard time. We shouldn't judge.'

'What kind of hard time?' Rob asked.

'Who knows? Something to do with the girl's dad, folks say. They came to the island as a place to hide. Off the radar, like.' Rob's dad slowed the truck to avoid a stupid lamb lying on the road.

'They'd settle better if they joined in island life. It takes more than one person to raise a child. It's not good for the girl to be left alone so much.'

'She's got her dog for company,' I said.

I forgot about Mara once we were at Rob's. I mucked about with Rob and Euan and a football on the Mackenzies' field. We sat on the wall, after, and Euan told us about the lambs and the shearers, and Rob's mum made us eggs and beans on toast for tea. Rob's dad drove me home.

We went past the lochan. There was no sign of Mara or Django.

'You're quiet,' Mum said, later that evening. 'You missing Dad?'

I nodded. It was easier to let her think that.

'He's looking for a different job,' Mum said. 'One that will mean he can live here with us all the time. I know it's hard for you, Jamie. Fee hates it. Wishes we'd never come. Do you, too?'

'Never,' I said, truthfully. 'I love it here. Don't you?'

'Yes, I do. But is it selfish of me?'

I didn't know what to say to that. 'I'm off to bed.'

'OK. Sleep tight. Mind the bugs don't—'

I hopped up the stairs two at a time, fast.

Up in my bedroom under the eaves I listened to the sea turning, and the gulls calling. A curlew flew over the field, its burble of sad, lonely notes floating on the wind. I thought of Mara in her faded blue swimsuit, ankle-deep in the lochan, waiting for me.

I'd let her down. Maybe that had happened to her lots of times, before, and that was why she didn't go to school or have any other friends.

I thought about me.

Scared to swim, scared to be friends with a girl who was just a bit different. Scared to be me.

Swimming

The next morning, I got up as soon as I heard Mum clattering in the kitchen. We had breakfast together. She talked to Dad on the phone. I waited for her to leave the house, then I got my bike out, and grabbed my backpack with the towel. I'd made my mind up.

The lochan was shiny in the sun that early morning. No one was about. The road was empty in both directions. The duck family dabbled among the reeds, all seven ducklings together with the mother duck.

I slid down the bank, pulled off my trainers and stripped down to my swimming shorts, and paddled along the edge. My feet sank into the silty mud and it squidged between my toes. I tried not to think about leeches and bloodsuckers. I waded deeper. There were stones to stand on. Safe enough. I got used to the cold. I watched a fallen leaf spin on the surface. *Do it*, I told myself. *Don't think.* I counted to ten. I took a deep breath and made myself slide under.

I gasped. The water was dead cold. But it felt silky-soft and smooth, not salty and stingy like sea-water. I could see all the way down through the golden peaty water to the stones at the bottom. I took one foot off the bottom, put my arms out, let the water slip over my shoulders. I lifted the other foot. I was actually floating. Swimming, now.

I did a kind of splashy doggy-paddle. I must have been holding my breath, because suddenly I'd run out of air. I stopped to take big gulps. I paddled on again with my head up out of the water, and after a while I could breathe and paddle at the same time. I stayed really close to the shore, so shallow I kept bumping my knees on the stones. I went a bit deeper, and it got easier. No one was watching. No one was criticizing the way I swam or telling me to breathe in a different way or turning it into a competition. I kept stopping, just to check how deep I was, to feel the stones firm under my feet, but in all I swam the whole edge of the lochan. I guess it wasn't really far, maybe the same as one length of a swimming pool, but for me that was pretty amazing.

When I got out, my legs were red with cold and I was shivering but I'd done it. Tomorrow I would do it again. And the day after. I'd keep practising, and then I'd try swimming in the sea. And then I would show Mara.

If she was speaking to me.

She didn't come to the boat shed that day or the next two.

'What's happened to the lass?' Grandpa asked me on the third day. 'She was coming along so well. I had her down as a sticker, not a quitter.'

Mid-morning, when we had our break, I looked out through the window at the back of the shed, and there was Mara's boat, scudding across the bay, back and forth. She was having a great time without me.

Grandpa saw her too. He sighed.

'She could learn the trade, earn a decent amount, if she kept at it,' Grandpa said. 'She could be an apprentice here, instead of larking about like a wild thing.' He smoothed his hand along the edge of the boat he was building. 'Beautiful,' he said. 'A fine piece of craftsmanship, though I say it myself. She's looking pretty good.'

'Why do you call the boat *she*?'

'That's the tradition. I suppose because most sailors were *he*. And the relationship between the sailor and the boat is very particular and special, like lovers.'

I squirmed at those words coming out of Grandpa's mouth.

'Maybe a girl sailor or boat builder would call her boat he.' Grandpa smiled. He handed me a sheet of rough-grained sandpaper and a wooden block. 'Wrap the paper round the block; it makes it easier to get a good steady stroke along the edges. You want the wood finish to feel like silk.'

I sanded the boat ribs; Mara skittered back and forth across the bay in *Stardust*. My boat shed day seemed longer than usual.

At half past three Grandpa told me it was time to stop. 'Get out in the sun, lad. Make the most of it while it lasts.'

I cycled along the shore road. A thin wisp of smoke curled up from the beach. I followed the smoke and the smell of burning.

I saw Django, first, chasing gulls along the sand. The boat was anchored in the bay. I found Mara further up the beach, feeding bits of dried dune grass into her smoky fire. She'd made a heap of driftwood but most of it was too damp to burn. And she was shoving paper into the flames. The wind gusted and whirled ashy fragments of paper along the sand. I could see print—bits of letter—brown envelope.

'You're burning letters?'

Mara's cheeks were red from the fire.

I remembered what Rob's dad had said the other day. Perhaps they were letters from her dad.

She scowled. 'Horrible letters. Best got rid of.'

I crouched down to fuss Django. 'Letters from who?'

'The Council. The Education Authority. The Mrs-Make-Children-Miserable. That's who.'

'What do you mean? What are you talking about, Mara?'

Her eyes were fierce and shiny-bright. 'Letters about school. Making me go.' She spat the words.

It's not so bad, I wanted to say. *You might even like it.*

I kept my mouth shut.

I helped her get the fire going strong. I found some dry old fence posts at the top of the dunes, and at last we got the flames leaping.

Mara did a war dance round the fire. She sang a made-up song that hardly sounded like words at all. She was wild and strange and scary.

Django chased and barked.

I fed the fire with wood, kept it burning steadily. Mara danced on.

Off with the faeries, Mum would say.

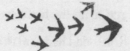

'Did you go to school when you were little?' I asked, when she finally sat down. I thought she might blow up again, but she went quiet.

'Mum taught me to read and write. We lived in . . . another country.' She shivered. 'I never went to an actual school.'

'So you don't really know what it's like,' I said. 'You could try it.'

Mara's face went pale. 'I'd have to go away *all week*,' she said. 'Live with strangers. *Be* with people all day. Be inside all the time, like a prison.'

'You don't have to go *away* to school till the year you turn fourteen,' I told her. 'Fee will be going there for the first time when school starts up again in August. But our island school's fine. It's small. The people are nice. You could make new friends.' I took a deep breath. 'I'd be there.'

Mara narrowed her eyes at me. 'I *am* fourteen this year. That's the whole point.'

Duh. Stupid me or what?

But she did look much younger than that. She was nothing like Fee or her friends. Megan. Suze. It was hard to imagine Mara in the same class as them. And yes, she would be totally miserable. I understood that. It would be like me, in my old school.

'What did the letters say?'

'That I'm not attending school. No evidence I am learning at the required levels. That it is a legal requirement I receive an education. Or they will take my mum to court.'

'But burning the letters won't stop them, will it?'

'What, then?' she snapped.

'I dunno. Get proof that you do learn stuff? Grandpa could tell them about you learning to make boats . . . And you can sail, and know the names of birds and shells and things. You can make a fire . . . ' I trailed off. It sounded hopeless even to me.

There wasn't anything I could say to help.

We sat quietly and the sea shooshed in and out. Django rested his head on her lap.

The flames died down. The embers glowed red hot. 'Our fire's perfect for cooking on, now,' I said. 'We should get sausages.'

'Or fish,' Mara said. 'We can catch some.'

'How?'

'Off the boat, of course. Come on.' She was already racing down the beach. As soon as she was moving she seemed happy again.

I found some big stones and put them around the fire to keep it safe. I put the thickest driftwood log on the fire. It was damp, but it would smoulder slowly and keep the fire alight while we were away.

Mara was already preparing the oars, pulling up the anchor chain. I rolled up my jeans and waded out to join her.

On the boat, Mara came truly alive. Sure of herself. Of course she was older than me; I saw that now.

She opened a box full of fishing things—lures and flies and hooks. She showed me how to cast. She was better at it than my dad. She knew the best place to go for fish, near the rocks but not so near that a wave could bash the boat into them. We caught three silver mackerel, and we cooked them over the fire, and we stayed till the sun went and it got too cold to sit outside any longer. The breeze and the smoke kept the midges at bay.

'Will you leave the boat here overnight?' I asked her.

'No way! I'll sail her back round to our home beach,' Mara said.

'Isn't it too windy?'

'It's in the right direction,' Mara said. 'I'll be fine.'

'How will you get the boat onto shore by yourself?'

She looked at me with a kind of scorn. 'How do you think? I did it hundreds of times before you turned up, Jamie.'

Of course she did. But it still seemed a lonely thing, to me.

I walked back home. I imagined Mara turning up at that wooden shack where there was no electric or hot water. I imagined her mum sitting at the table, painting bits of wood and pebble. I imagined the quiet, and the darkness as night fell.

All the lights were on in our house, and music was thumping out through the open windows upstairs. Fee's bedroom. Voices. I recognized Suze's. A sleepover? My heart sank.

Fee clattered downstairs and put her arm across to block my way up. 'Mum's out and I'm in charge. You have to stay downstairs in the kitchen and OUT OF MY ROOM, and no listening. You were supposed to be here for dinner so you are already in big trouble.'

I stuck my tongue out at her. 'Why've you got make-up all

over your face? You look stupid. And you can't stop me going into my room, so there.' I pushed past her.

She shrieked as if I had hurt her on purpose.

Suze and two other girls appeared on the landing. 'Hi Jamie,' they chorused. They all had make-up on. Tight clothes. Heels. I imagined them tottering along the island road, and it made me want to laugh.

I went into my bedroom and shut the door, and tried not to hear their racket for the rest of the evening. They were talking about their new school, and the lush boys they'd meet there, and all the amazing things they'd do and how exciting it would be, living together in dorms all week . . . blah blah blah.

I leaned out of the window, and breathed in island air, and listened to the curlew and the skylarks and the sound of the sea washing in over the sand on the beach. The lights at the harbour mouth came on: one red, one green, to guide boats in at night. The fishing boats would return on the high tide with their catch of lobster and scallops and langoustines. Maybe I could get a job doing that, one day, if it turned out I wasn't good enough to be a boat builder like Grandpa.

Mara would be good enough. Grandpa had already said so.

Maybe he could teach her maths as well as how to build boats.

Maybe we could read books and write stories together for English, and she wouldn't have to go away to school after all . . .

Fee and her friends were still crashing around, dancing and having a good time. I tried to imagine Mara going to school with them and it was impossible.

I lay on top of the bed. My head ached from too much thinking. My clothes still smelled of charred fish and wood smoke. It had been fun, cooking on a fire on the beach. I'd tell Dad about the fish.

Mum got home about eleven. I heard her laughing with Fee and the other girls. The wind buffeted the open window. I leaned on the sill to look out. The red and green harbour lights winked in the semi-darkness of the summer night. The waves turned. I watched a short-eared owl quarter the field, hunting on silent wings, seeming almost to float.

This was my life, now.

I remembered lying on my bed back in the old house: the sounds of the city, the feeling of buildings all around, pressing in, and the sickness in my belly whenever I thought of school. Adam Roberts' taunts in the playground. The smell of the dinner hall. The too-high windows in Miss Piper's classroom, framing a grey sky. Homework. Uniform. Spelling tests. Tests.

Tests. Tests. Each school day, it was like I was slowly sinking underwater. Drowning.

Summer was speeding by too fast.

It was already August. Only ten days or so till school started up again. That was why Mara had been so furious. Desperate. For Mara, time was running out.

Eight

Thursday. It was the morning of the annual Island Agricultural Show.

Fee and I carried Mum's plastic boxes full of crab and salad rolls over to the car. We dumped them in the boot.

'Thank you, darlings.' Mum surveyed the stack. 'That should be plenty. We'll make some money if they all sell. Hop in, then, gorgeous girl.' She made a funny face behind Fee's back.

I laughed.

Fee was all dressed up with make-up and tight jeans and a new top. It was a miracle that she was coming along. But according to her, *literally everyone* goes to the show. It's the big social event of the summer. All her new friends would be there. *Fit boys* from some of the other islands, too (her words, not mine).

'Why don't you come in the car with us?' Mum asked me.

'I'll ride my bike over,' I said. 'Then I can leave when I want.'

I watched the car bump down our track, stop to pick up Granny and Grandpa, and drive on again. A whole stream of cars—at least five—followed along the single-track road.

I cycled to the beach, first. No sign of anyone. A skein of geese flew across the bay, honking loudly, and l watched them land on a patch of machair. Fifteen geese. Greylags. Mara had taught me that. She'd taught me lots of things, I realized—the different birds, the names of wild plants. She helped me to notice the small details—how many different kinds of wild flowers in just one small patch of machair. A patch of corn marigolds. Purple vetch. Marsh orchids. Clover. Because of her, I was getting better at swimming. Less scared of the water. I'd been practising most days. I'd sailed the boat. I was changing.

The sea would be freezing but I'd made up my mind. I dumped the bike in the dunes, stripped off down to my shorts and ran into the water. I ducked under, quick, teeth chattering, swam a few metres, hardly breathing, almost sick with the cold. It got a bit easier, mainly because I'd gone totally numb.

I swam along close to the beach, and back, and ran out again, shaking my hair like a wet Django, and I ran up and down the sand until the blood started running again and I could feel warmth tingle down my legs and arms. My fingers and feet were blue-white. I dried myself and put on all my clothes and still I was cold to the core, but I'd done it. Swum in the sea by myself and survived.

I found the remains of yesterday's fire. Ashes. I picked up a tiny fragment of paper, singed by the fire but still with writing on it. A name, it looked like. *Papai?* I put it in my jacket pocket.

I cycled past the queue of cars and trucks waiting to get into the Show at Horta.

'Hey, Jamie!' Rob called as I wheeled past the sheep pens. He and Euan were watching the sheep judging, each with a dog on a lead (Dog Show, 1.45 p.m., the poster said). They'd dressed up too: smart clothes, combed hair.

'Just getting some food,' I yelled back. I went to beg a crab roll off Mum in the tea tent.

'Tea? Coffee? Hot chocolate, Jamie?' Granny was in charge

of Teas and Hot Drinks. She smoothed down my damp hair and hugged me.

'This is our eldest grandson,' she said to the lady taking the money. 'James. Mrs Shelagh Stuart.'

I shook hands. I knew I'd gone red. The lady said I looked like my grandpa. 'A chip off the old block, eh?' She laughed.

Granny handed me a cup of hot chocolate. 'Off you go now and enjoy yourself,' she said. She wouldn't let me pay.

I went over to watch the sheep judging with Rob and Euan. The man who'd played the fiddle at the ceilidh was talking into the microphone, announcing the next breed to be judged, cracking jokes in Gaelic.

'Are you showing your special sheep?' I asked Euan.

'Nah, our little Hebrideans are too shy and flighty,' he said. 'But Mam's showing folk how to hand spin the wool and that, in the marquee.'

We went to look around.

We got free strawberries off Rob's granny. Two tubs each, with cream and sugar. We looked at the chickens and ducks in hutches. First prize: the black cockerel. He was pretty pleased with himself, showing off, crowing loudly. The baking and home-grown-produce judging was still going on in the barn so they wouldn't let us in. 'Guess the weight of the dumpling, for charity,' the man at the door said. 'Three goes for a pound.'

Rob fished out a pound from his pocket. We guessed wildly. None of us had a clue.

'So, what's the prize?' Rob asked.

'The dumpling, of course!'

We hooted with laughter. 'Hope we don't win, then!' Euan said. The dumpling was this massive pudding, full of lard and currants. It looked disgusting.

We wandered through the arts and crafts tent to see what free stuff there was. There were stalls selling pottery mugs and jugs at ridiculous prices, and oil paintings of sea views; lots of knitted things. Someone was trying to flog ugly orange wellies. And right at the end of the marquee, near the field, Mara's mum sat at a table. No one was talking to her. All the other stallholders were chatting and laughing, but it was like there was a kind of silent force field around her.

I ducked away.

Too late. She'd spotted me. She waved madly. 'Hi, Jamie. How are you?'

I went a bit closer. 'Hi,' I said back, sheepish.

Rob put his hands in his pockets. I knew he was watching me.

She picked up one of the driftwood sculptures laid out on the turquoise cloth on her table. 'Remember this one?' She wafted a sea-horse-shaped thing at me.

Heat prickled round my neck. Oh no . . .

Euan and Rob muttered something. They slunk off out of the tent.

'I'll catch you up,' I called after them.

Mara's mum seemed oblivious to the effect she had on people. I was surprised she was here at all. But I guess she knew there would be tourists: money to be made.

'She's not here, if you're looking for Mara,' her mum said.

I didn't say that I wasn't. I didn't know what to say, really.

'Can I interest you in a pebble doorstop whale?' She picked up a large grey stone in both hands and held it out to me. 'Or a paperweight puffin, perhaps? Have one for free, Jamie.'

'Nah, I'm OK, thanks,' I said.

She looked disappointed. 'Come round again to see us soon, won't you? Come for tea. Come today if you like.'

'I can't today . . . '

'Tomorrow, another day, any day. We're always there!' She

flung her arms out wide and laughed in this strange way, like when your voice slips or breaks a bit.

'Got to go! My friends are waiting,' I said.

They were up at the field where the dog show was due to begin. I patted Euan's sheepdog. Mouse. She's called that because she was the runt of the litter—so small they didn't think she'd survive. But she did. Obviously.

She wagged her tail and gave me her paw. She's dead obedient, is Mouse. She likes to work. It makes her happy, Euan says. Most sheepdogs are like that. They need to be busy and active all the time.

'So,' Euan said. 'You going to tell us or what?'

'What?'

'We've seen you and that girl, Jamie. Everyone has. And that was the mother, the crazy hippy with the dreads. So, what's going on?'

I shrugged. 'Nothing. I see Mara on the beach sometimes. I had a go on her boat, once, that's all. She comes to my grandpa's boat shed sometimes, to learn.'

Euan laughed.

I bent down and patted Mouse again to hide my face.

'What's she like?' Rob asked. 'Is she as weird as she looks?'

I took a deep breath. 'No. She's OK. Grandpa says she's clever at learning about boatbuilding. She's just alone a lot, I guess.'

'Do you fancy her?'

'Shut up!' I shoved Euan hard and he shoved me back and before I knew it we were fighting and punching. I hit his chin with my fist and he grabbed me by the hair. His dog barked and jumped up and joined in.

'Break it up, man!' Rob pulled us apart.

We glared at each other.

'The dog show is about to begin,' a woman's voice called through a microphone. 'Take your places everyone. Class one, Obedience.'

Euan rubbed his chin. He shook himself out. He picked up the lead he'd dropped earlier. Mouse trotted at his heels towards the entrance to the dog show. He didn't look back or speak to me.

Rob shrugged.

'I'm off,' I said. 'See ya around.' I tried not to show how much it hurt.

I wheeled my bike over the rough grass, weaving through the crowds of people. Fee was sitting with a group of girls on the grass outside the tea tent, eyeing up the boys. She didn't notice me.

That girl called Wren waved.

I kept my head down.

I was shaking. I don't ever fight. How did that happen?

Flight

I cycled to Compass Hill. I wanted to be high up. I wanted air and space and time to think.

I cycled most of the way up the road that winds around to the top of the hill, left the bike against the stone wall and scrambled over the grass. No one was around. Distant voices from the show drifted up from the valley below. Music and tannoy announcements. I lay down on the grass and let my heart steady.

The sky was a dome of brilliant blue. Hardly a cloud. Not much wind. The air was clear. Bees hummed on the wild flowers and grasses. Purple clover. Yellow trefoil. Tufts of creamy meadowsweet scented the air with honey. Mara had taught me those names. My head pounded.

Gradually I calmed down.

I propped myself up on my elbows so I could look out to sea. Today was so clear and bright I could see the fishing islands. I saw the fine white line of surf breaking over the reef. And further out, far on the horizon but still clear, there were more islands. I stared. Blinked. Could hardly believe what I was seeing.

For the first time ever, I saw the dark shapes of the islands of St Kilda.

Before, they'd existed only in my imagination, a kind of story place. How was it possible? They were sixty-five kilometres away. But I recognized the shapes: the massive sheer cliffs of Dun, Soay, Boreray, Hirta. I'd seen the photos in Grandpa's book. At school we'd watched an old black and white film of the last people leaving the island forever.

A shiver rippled down my back.

I stood up. The road wound round higher to the top of Compass Hill to a cluster of low grey buildings surrounded by a barbed-wire fence. Mara had told me a telescope was up there for tourists to use, that time we sat on the hill in the rain.

I fetched the bike and pushed it up the steep road to the very top. A big sign said *Ministry of Defence: KEEP OUT*. But at the side of the road next to a stone wall was a big telescope like those ones you get at the seaside, which you have to slot money into. This one was free.

Even with the telescope the islands were too far off for me to see any detail. Dark shapes, silhouetted against the blue sky. The biggest island was like a mountain, sticking straight up from the sea. It really was like looking at the edge of the world. Blue sea glittered in the sunlight.

I moved the telescope round to look at our island. Fields. Stone walls. Farms, crofts, small houses scattered over the island. Cars parked on the field at Horta. The marquee and animal pens.

I scanned the coast towards the west. There was Rob's croft, and Euan's farm. The black dots of Hebridean sheep in the field. A flock of geese grazing the same grass. I traced the track along the dunes, and thought I could make out the wooden shack that was Mara's home. And that was the beach where she sailed from.

My eyes strained in the bright sunlight. The light off the sea was dazzling. I blinked, and checked again. Was that someone on the beach? And a boat? Could it be? I tried to focus the telescope again. The image seemed to shift and shimmer as I looked. But there was definitely a figure on the beach, and a boat, and something running about—a small dog.

It must be Mara.

What was she doing?

She seemed to be putting things onto the boat. Boxes? Bags? She was packing the boat for a journey. She was leaving when she knew everyone was busy with the show. Her mother would be away from home all day.

I remembered that day when she asked Grandpa all those questions about sailing to the fishing islands. If I had noticed the fine weather today, the clear view of the islands, the gentlest roar of surf on the reef, the perfect wind and tide for sailing out to them, she would have, too.

She'd reckoned that no one would see her go.

The surf might not be pounding right now, but the weather could change in a moment. Grandpa had told her how danger-ous it was to go through the reef. It could be deadly.

I had to stop her.

Part Two: The Journey

I Didn't Mean to Go to Sea

I whizzed downhill on the bike. Would I get there before she sailed off? It was maddening how slowly I had to go along the rough track between the machair fields to get to the dunes and Mara's beach. *No punctures! Please no punctures.*

Almost there. I jumped off, flung the bike down at the edge of the track next to the line of dunes, clambered up the sand between the scratchy stems of marram grass. I found the abandoned boat trailer, Mara's footprints and Django's scuffed pawprints in the soft sand. I half ran, half slid down the dunes the other side onto the beach.

Mara's boat *Stardust* bobbed on the waves, sideways on to the wind, as Mara adjusted the sails ready for her voyage.

I didn't call out. The moment she saw me she'd speed up, sail away. Laughing, most likely, waving goodbye. But I knew I had a few seconds before she spotted me, because all she'd be able to hear right now was the sailcloth flapping in the wind, and the breaking surf, and Django, yapping. She had her back to the beach, bent over as she untied the rope.

I pulled off my trainers and waded out, moving fast as I could against the breaking waves, deeper. A bigger wave broke right on me, almost knocking me over. Now I was drenched, and the sea was freezing, of course, but I kept going, wading deeper. I needed to grab the stern of the boat before the next wave broke, or she saw me.

Django was going mad, barking and wagging his tail in excitement and running up and down the deck. It was the dog that eventually made Mara turn.

Her face.

Astonished.

Furious.

'What are you DOING?' she yelled. 'Get back! It's not safe, Jamie. You're in too deep!' She grabbed the tiller with one hand; with the other she pulled the sail tight, trying to get the boat to ride the waves rather than being flooded as they broke.

I grabbed the side of the boat, felt the solid wood, and then pain as she peeled my fingers off and pushed me away.

Next minute, another massive wave broke, swamped the boat, washed right over me, filled my mouth. For a moment all I saw was water, deep, cold, terrible deep water. I couldn't breathe. The wave tumbled me over, dragged me down. I didn't know which way was up.

No breath.

Sand, water, darkness.

Pressure on my head, on my shoulders and in my chest, like nothing I've felt before.

A moment of terrible stillness, as if everything had stopped. This was it. The thing I'd most feared all my life. And then all was movement again, and I surfaced, took a shuddering breath.

Next thing, I felt Mara's strong hand clutch mine. I clung on to her. Now instead of pushing me away she was pulling me hard, hauling me over the edge of the boat. Relief flooded me as I felt the solid wood of the boat deck, and air above. I had survived. I wasn't going to drown. But I was freezing, shaking, huddled on the floor of the boat in a wet heap.

The wind was filling the sails and now the boat was scudding, fast, out to sea. All Mara's attention was on steering the boat, judging which way the waves would break, trying to make sure we didn't capsize.

I heaved myself up just in time and sicked up salt water over the edge of the boat. It made my guts hurt and my throat burned and I thought I'd never stop. All I wanted was to be back on the beach. For Mara to turn the boat and sail us back to shore.

Not the faintest chance of that. She kept steadily sailing out to sea, her mouth fixed and determined, refusing to look at or speak to me.

And I was too scared and sick and weak to say or do anything. I lay there in a heap until I could breathe again and my lungs stopped burning. In a daze I put on the life jacket she chucked at me from the locker under the seat. My fingers fumbled to fasten the tabs. I shivered. Big shuddering shakes racked my whole body.

The boat steadied. We were over the breaking, messy bit of sea. It smoothed out. Mara relaxed. The sail flapped a bit, and she steered back into the wind. I listened to the sound of the water rushing under the bows. We were sailing fast.

'I don't know what you were trying to do,' Mara said at last. 'A stowaway? Coming along for the thrill of the ride?'

Was she actually laughing?

When I'd very nearly drowned?

'You're OK,' she said. 'You swallowed some sea, that's all. You'll warm up now the sun's on you.'

Her eyes narrowed. She was staring at something ahead. She checked the compass fixed on the boat, and then the sea chart spread out on the seat at her side. She was plotting her course.

'We line these rocks up, and then we'll aim due west for the gap in the reef,' she said, as if that was a perfectly normal thing to do on a Thursday afternoon.

'It's too dangerous,' I stuttered. 'Grandpa said so.'

'But the truth is, he did it a hundred times,' Mara said. 'In the right conditions. With the right boat. Like us. We can do it, Jamie. Even better, now there's two of us.'

Django came to sit close to me. His body was warm against my cold legs. He licked my hand. For a second, tears came in my eyes. I really had thought I might die, just those few seconds underwater. And now I was heading out to the reefs with crazy Mara, like it or not. I might nearly die all over again. I might actually die.

Django understood.

Maybe Mara did too, in her own way. Her voice softened. 'Are you feeling better? Less sick?'

I nodded.

'You were trying to stop me, weren't you? But how did you even know what I was planning?' She frowned. 'Were you stalking me again, Jamie Mackinnon?'

'What do you mean, again?'

'Well, think about it. You seem to turn up wherever I go . . . and today of all days? What were you doing? Coincidence, or what?'

'I saw you from Compass Hill.'

'How come? That's not even possible.'

'Through that telescope. By chance.'

The boat lurched and we both had to cling on. Mara steered away from the wind and the sail flapped.

'You weren't at the show?' Mara asked,

'I was, but I'd had enough—anyway, I went up the hill, and I decided to look at the islands through the telescope—and then I saw you packing the boat and I guessed what you were doing. So I came to stop you. It's not safe, Mara. Supposing we can't get back again?'

'I've brought provisions. Food, and a blanket and sleeping bag and fishing stuff and water and everything I need. I'm not coming back. That's the point.'

I stared at her. 'What are you saying?' I had to shout above the roar of the sea.

'I'm running away. Going to live there in one of the old stone houses. Fish. Then no one can make me go to stupid school.'

'You've gone completely bonkers, Mara. How can you possibly think that can work? Your mother will be mad with worry when she realizes you haven't come home. And what about me?'

'Well, you weren't part of the plan, were you? That's your fault, for messing it up.'

I stood up, and staggered as the boat tipped. A wave broke over the bows and trickled back over the seats.

'SIT DOWN!' she yelled. 'You idiot! Have you forgotten everything I taught you?'

Now I realized why the roar of the sea was so loud. The reef was just ahead of us, and what from a distance had seemed a thin line of surf was now a turning, tumbling mass of white water.

Bile rose in my throat. I retched. 'Turn the boat, Mara!' I yelled. 'Take us BACK!' But my voice was lost in the pounding surf. Mara couldn't hear a word.

Django crept closer to me. He pressed himself against my leg. I felt him trembling.

I shut my eyes.

The Reef

The roar of the surf filled my whole body. Even the air itself smelled different: colder and sharper. It was as if everything now focused on the line of rocks, and the gap we were heading towards. Beyond, I saw a stretch of deeper, calmer water. Navy blue. As soon as we reached that, we'd be fine. But supposing we didn't? Suppose we hit the rocks, instead?

'JAMIE!' Mara yelled. 'Go up front and tell me how close we are to the rocks. How deep the water is. NOW!'

I crawled forward, my stomach heaving.

Django cowered and trembled under the wooden seat. 'It's OK,' I told him. 'You'll be all right.'

I edged forward, held on to the mast with one hand, and leaned forwards so I was lying on the front bit of the deck. I was soaked with spray. The surf pounded and roared. I kept my eyes fixed on the gap in the rocks: it came and went as the waves rolled in, so that sometimes it was clear as a way through, and the next second was impossible to see—there was no break in the rocks, in the heaving surf.

'How deep?' Mara yelled again. 'Are we clear of the rocks?'

How deep? I couldn't tell. The water was too churned up.

'We're really close,' I yelled back.

Mara shouted something but I couldn't hear. I turned, and saw her face, ablaze with excitement.

She grinned and shouted again. 'Hold on tight! Going through after the next big wave.'

There was no time to think or speak. The wave rolled in, crashed over the rocks in a mass of wild, white foaming water, lifted the boat, and then came a tiny lull, as it rolled on. 'NOW!' I yelled, as the gap appeared again.

Mara saw it too, and in that second she steered the boat and tightened the sail so the wind took it and swept us through. It happened so fast I didn't have time to hold my breath.

We were so close to the line of rock I could have reached out and touched the jagged black sides, and below us, as the water smoothed, I saw more rock beneath us, only a metre or so below. I remembered what Mara taught me before, about the centreboard, and the danger of catching it on the bottom and breaking it off, so I yanked it up. It took both hands, and all my strength. The boat rocked horribly. And then by some miracle we were through the rocks and sailing out the other side.

'Brilliant!' Mara shouted.

I lowered the board again, felt the boat steady.

Mara grinned.

I'd done the right thing for once.

The wind seemed stronger this side of the reef. We'd got safely through, but this was just the beginning. Now there were miles of open water, and only the remote fishing islands ahead, and no sign of the shore, or other boats—and Mara had never been this far before, either. We were out at sea, alone, at the whim of the weather and the tides. No wind, and we'd be stuck. Too much, and we could capsize, or be swept off course.

And no one knew we were here.

Mara didn't care. She'd planned this all along. The only bit she hadn't planned was me being with her too.

I'd never considered, before, how in a sailing boat out in the ocean you can't ever stop to have a rest or a break. You have to keep on sailing. As long as the wind keeps blowing, you keep going.

'Find yourself something warm in my bag,' Mara said.

Her dry bag was tied under the wooden seat. I fumbled with numb fingers to untie it and open the clasp. I rummaged for a jumper and hoiked out her big blue woollen one. 'This OK?'

She nodded.

It wasn't much too big. It was warm and thick at least, and there was no one to laugh at me wearing a girl's jumper. The sleeves could be like gloves as well. But my legs were still freezing.

'The most dangerous thing about sailing in these waters is getting too cold and tired,' Mara said. 'You make bad decisions 'cause your brain stops working properly.'

'Well great,' I said. 'Mine stopped working a long time ago.'

She laughed.

'It's not funny. I haven't got any proper warm clothes. It's not safe. I don't want to be sailing out here. You have to take me back.'

'Too late,' Mara said. 'Look at the surf now, on the reef. No way I'm going through that!'

She was right, of course. The waves were huge, breaking right over the reef. The tide and current made it impossible to try now.

'It's OK, calm down,' Mara said. 'We'll aim for the little harbour your grandpa told us about, on the eastern side of Heisker. We can land there and make a fire and get warm. You might even enjoy yourself, Jamie.'

I sat hunched in the bows, one hand on Django, the other clinging on to the mast. I didn't say anything. I watched the horizon, and even that made me feel sick because the boat dipped and dropped with each wave and nothing stayed level, and my teeth chattered, and I hated myself for getting into this stupid mess in the first place.

We went on like that for ages.

Then maybe the wind direction changed, just a little. It slackened off. The sun came out. The sea calmed; it went from dark and foamy and terrifying to a turquoise blue, sparkling with sunlight. The boat stopped bucking and tipping so much. I started noticing seabirds, and tiny silver fish swimming in shoals just under our bows.

'Gannets!' Mara shouted.

There were loads of them, with their massive wings. When

they dived for fish they plunged from the sky like white arrows.

'Razorbills, and puffins, too.' Mara pointed as they flew low over the water in front of us.

The little boat pushed bravely forward. My head was full of sound: the rhythmic slap of water under the bows, the flapping sails, the cry of seabirds. Everything else emptied out. It was like a kind of letting-go of everything else—all my normal world disappeared.

Like flicking a switch: that was the moment I stopped hating everything and being so scared. And maybe it was because I'd really thought I was going to drown, back there, but had somehow survived. I realized I didn't need to be so scared any more.

Now, we were explorers, adventurers, on a journey to somewhere new and thrilling.

Mara must have seen the change in me. 'Can you take the helm for bit, Jamie?' she asked. 'Just hold the tiller still: keep us going in the same direction, west-north-west on the compass.'

I shuffled back to swap places with her. I took the tiller and felt it twitch under my hand, like a living thing.

She watched for a while, to check I was doing it right.

'Hungry?' she asked.

I nodded.

She rummaged in one of the boxes. 'Ta da!' She passed me a slab of chocolate and gave Django one of his special biscuits. He curled himself back under the bench. 'Not so far now,' she told him. He thumped his tail on the wooden deck. He was trying to be brave.

'How far, do you reckon?' I asked. I no longer had to shout, now everything had calmed down.

She screwed up her eyes to stare at the sea ahead.

The islands were there, low dark shapes, but hardly clearer than when I looked through the telescope up on Compass Hill.

'Further than I thought,' Mara said.

At Sea

Out at sea the light plays tricks. One minute it seemed we were making good progress, the next, the islands looked as far off as ever. You can't simply sail in a straight line; depending on the wind, you have to zigzag, to keep the wind in the sails, which makes it take twice as long. And then there was the tide, and the current. The tide was still going out, pulling us out to sea, but the current was a different thing. It tugged us sideways, and it was unpredictable.

We took it in turns to be at the helm. Mara was exhausted. I figured I needed to do my proper share of holding the tiller and managing the sails, to give her a break. And it was fine because it wasn't so windy any more, and the waves were steady and not too big.

Mara shouted directions. There was so much to think about all at once, like watching the wind on the water, and keeping the sails taut, and adjusting the tiller to follow the course on the compass, and working out when to gybe.

'See!' Mara said. 'You can do it. You've totally learned to sail, Jamie. Your grandpa would be proud.'

'My grandpa would be furious,' I said. 'Us, sailing away without telling anyone? Going through the dangerous reef? Me not properly equipped with warm clothes and stuff? He'd be fuming!' I corrected myself. 'He WILL be furious, when he finds out.'

'Ah. But by then we will have sailed safely to the islands and camped and lived there and been totally self-sufficient on fish and the stuff I packed, and proved we can do it,' Mara said. 'So he won't have a leg to stand on.'

There was something wrong with her logic. A lot wrong. But I didn't bother to tell her that. I was having too good a time.

Closer up, the islands looked magical. Now we could see grassy slopes and old stone houses where people once lived, and where fishermen used to stay when they got stuck on the island in bad weather. I imagined us camping in one of the houses—or two houses, one each, and making a fire and catching fish to barbecue. It seemed possible, now. Mara showed me some of the stuff she'd brought: a blanket, and a sleeping bag, and tins of beans, and bread and cheese, matches, a cooking pan. And dog biscuits. A huge carton of dog crunchies.

'If we're desperate, we can eat those,' I teased her. 'Full of protein!'

The harbour was on the eastern side, Grandpa had told Mara, away from the prevailing westerly winds and sheltered from storms. We still couldn't see it. This side seemed to be nothing but rock. Sheer, black rock.

'I expect when we get really close we'll see the gap,' I said. 'A proper stone-walled harbour entrance. We're just too far off to see it yet.'

Mara stood up and the boat wobbled. She went forward and leaned over the bows to check the depth of the water. 'Turn her out of the wind,' she called back. 'We need to slow right down.'

Tricky. The wind seemed to push the sail, and made the boat judder. It felt unbalanced, like we might tip right over. 'You take the helm, Mara!' I yelled. 'I'll do the depth sounding. Swap places.'

She didn't hear at first. The sail was flapping too much. She was peering at the rock face, searching.

'Should we take down the sails?' I shouted. 'MARA!'

The boat lurched and she turned to face me.

'You take over. Please, Mara?'

She came forward and swapped places with me. My hands were cramped from holding the tiller so tight.

'I still can't see any way in. We'll have to sail round to the other side of the big island,' she said.

'Why?'

'We can land on one of the sandy beaches, like we do at home.'

'But how do you know there *are* sandy beaches?'

'There's bound to be, on the west side. Same as our island. Rocky east, sandy west.'

Django whimpered. He sat up. He looked cold and miserable, as if all he wanted to do was get off the boat onto proper firm land. I was beginning to feel like that too. We'd seemed so close to landing, and now we had to sail on round the islands. And what if Mara's sandy beaches weren't there after all? She was only guessing.

I crept forward to the bows and leaned out. The water was so clear I could see right down to the rocky bottom, and the purple blobs of sea anenomes, and tiny fish, and weed and thick kelp like a lush underwater garden. The sort of sea garden that otters like. Any other time, and we might have watched for otters . . .

'We could row round,' I said. 'Might that be easier?'

Mara frowned. 'No way. The tide and the current are much too strong.'

We both knew sailing close to rocks was dangerous. A gust of wind or a big wave can take you right onto them, and break the boat . . .

Never broken in a sea. I heard Grandpa's voice, as if right in my ear.

But that phrase was about the boats *he* built. The traditional ones made at the shed by my family going back generations. *Stardust* wasn't one of those boats, specially designed and made for these seas. And Mara was thirteen. Not even an islander, really. She'd come from somewhere else. She'd never sailed this far out before. And what if we crashed onto the rocks?

I glanced at her face; her mouth was set firm and stubborn. I knew that look. Not to be argued with.

Her hair was all tangled up by wind and spray into a funny kind of bird's nest.

'What you smiling at?' she snapped.

'Nothing.'

'Well, stop.'

Spiky, difficult Mara. It was her way of covering up fear. I saw it in her eyes, and the way she jiggled her foot. I'd seen it in her before.

And something shifted in me, then. A new kind of courage kicked in. It was as if there was only space for one person at a time to be frightened. This was Mara's turn. And so it was my turn not to be.

The sail flapped wildly as we came away from the shelter of the island. The boat seemed to tremble as Mara pulled it round. A gust of wind filled the sail; I dodged the boom as it swung across.

'Hold tight!' she yelled.

Django whimpered. He crawled under the bench and put his head on Mara's bag. 'Good dog,' I told him. 'You're OK.' He didn't lift his head or wag his tail. I thought of that phrase, *Sick as a dog*. Of course! That was what was wrong with him. Django was seasick.

Ahead, the surface of the sea was fretted silver-grey. 'Squall coming!' I called to Mara.

She moved the tiller, slackened the mainsail, the boat slowed down slightly and then everything shook and shuddered as the wind hit us and a wave broke over the boat.

I untied the bucket, scooped the water up, and emptied it over the side. I kept bailing for ages. Each breaking wave brought more water gushing into the boat.

The boat rode the next set of waves. Mara worked out how to judge each oncoming wave so we didn't take them head-on so often.

It was a kind of dance: wind, and wave, and boat. I saw how strong the boat was, how well Mara handled it even though she was afraid. I wasn't so worried we'd capsize or sink, any more. Just as long as we both stayed in the boat we'd be all right. Washed overboard, and that would be it . . .

But there wasn't far to go. Already, we were almost round the rocky south of the island. We'd sail round to the west, and find the long sandy beaches where we'd be able to go ashore.

'We'll make a fire,' I told Django. 'You can warm up soon.'

He stood up, sniffed the air, as if he could smell dry land at last.

'Nearly there!' I shouted to Mara. 'The water's shallower here. Best steer out a bit from the rocks.'

Mara changed tack. We came round the headland, and there, just as she predicted, was a long line of sandy beach, and waves breaking over a sandbar. We'd have to row the last bit of shallow water.

For a moment we were sailing fine, straight towards the sandbar. The sea seemed eerily calm. But the boat juddered, and we seemed to stop, and then we seemed to be dragged back, and we were moving fast away from the shore.

'What the—' Mara swore really loudly—I'd never heard her say words like that before.

'There's a rip,' she said.

Her voice was full of dread. 'A rip current. We're not going to be able to land. The rip is pulling us out to sea and there's nothing we can do.'

I stared at her.

The boat shuddered as we hit a wave rolling in towards the sandbar. I grabbed Django—he was standing on the bows, looking as if any moment he was going to swim for shore. Mara shouted at me to duck as the boom crashed round. I don't remember what happened next.

Too Far Out

B lue. Dazzling light.

Sunlight.

Bumping up, down, up . . .

Cool wind blowing on my face. Salt on my lips.

A sound—regular, like a loud heartbeat. Water, slapping wood.

The smell of damp.

Wet dog.

Shadow.

A dark shape. A bird, long neck stretched out, slow wing-flaps. My brain struggled to find the word for it.

Cormorant.

Gradually things stopped spinning.

'Phew. You're OK. How's your head?' Mara's voice. 'No, don't sit up. Keep still.'

My head.

A throbbing pain. I touched the bump just above my ear, felt the egg shape under the skin. Ouch.

'The boom,' Mara said, 'clocked you one.'

Now I remembered. It hurt to move my head. I lay still in the bottom of the boat.

We were sailing fast and smoothly. The sunlight made patterns on the sail, like ripples. For a while I lay there, watching the patterns curve and spiral and dance. My mind was empty. Peaceful. I dozed.

'Open your eyes,' Mara said. 'Stay awake now.'

I tried. I blinked, and focused on the mast, and the top of the sail, and the clouds scudding across the blue sky.

'You weren't out for long,' Mara said. 'Only a few seconds, probably. Luckily you fell into the boat and not OUT of it.' She was almost laughing. Perhaps it was the relief that I wasn't dead. Or maybe it had been funny, in her eyes.

I remembered more. The rip. 'And so—the island?'

'No way to land.'

'So, we . . . we're . . . ?'

'On our way to Newfoundland! Just a few thousand miles of ocean to go.'

'WHAT?'

'Just kidding, Jamie!'

'Not funny.'

I still couldn't work it out. 'So, you turned the boat round? We're going back home?'

Mara shook her head. 'Keep on to St Kilda, I reckon. It's a bit of a long way, but we'll be fine. People lived there for thousands of years. So, we can, too.'

I couldn't believe what I was hearing.

'It's sixty-five kilometres to St Kilda. Sheer cliffs. You need perfect weather to land. MARA!'

'What?'

'You're totally crazy! How can you even think that's possible? In this little boat? Us?'

'Why not?' A strip of sunlight caught her hair and face, and for a second she looked as if she was made of gold.

I sat up. Ahead of us, the sea stretched, calm and blue. The sky—well, that was blue too. Just a few high clouds. The sun was shining. It was more or less a perfect day for sailing to St Kilda.

A thrill of excitement curled in my belly and crept through my whole body.

We were sailing to St Kilda.

The sea was calm out here in the open water away from rocks or islands. I lay on my stomach on the bows, one hand trailing in the clear deep water, one on Django's damp fur. He stretched beside me and yawned. He seemed more settled. My head stopped hurting so much. My brain cleared.

Stardust sailed on, her white sails stretched taut and gleaming in the sun, and the water rushed steadily under the bows and made a swooshing sound that lulled Mara and me into a state of calm.

I took my turn at the helm. I watched the compass needle like a hawk, to keep us on course west. It was easy enough to see where we were heading. Not much chance of missing a set of islands that look like mountains, looming out of the water. And the wind kept steady but not too strong. The sea stayed calm. Our lucky day.

We talked, to pass the time. Hours of time. At least, Mara talked.

I'd not known her say so much before. She'd always seemed a private person, just getting on.

This was a different Mara.

She chatted about the place she lived when she was little, where her dad had a boat, and caught fish, and it was hot in summer and the winters were cold and snowy. She remembered hazy blue mountains, and vines in the garden, and chickens pecking about. White houses with red tiled roofs. Her granny standing in the sea in the hot evenings with her friends, all the old ladies talking to each other for hours, not swimming, just paddling in their big black bathing costumes, talking. And Mara herself swimming in the sea and helping her dad on the fishing boat. It sounded like she was happy.

'Why didn't you stay there?' I asked.

'Mum. She and my dad argued a lot. He shouted at her. She didn't like it.'

'What did he shout about?'

'Me. And how to do things, what to eat, how to live, who to be friends with. Money. Everything.'

She shivered. 'We left in a hurry, in the middle of the night. Well, it was dark, anyway. I don't know what time. I was little. Only seven. Mum woke me up and made me get dressed, and we drove off in a car, not our car, and then we were on a ferry to England. We couldn't tell my dad anything because he would have stopped us going.'

I tried to imagine that, but I couldn't.

'And we couldn't tell him where we went, Mum said, 'cause he would've come to get me, to take me back to the white house in the mountains.' Her voice caught. She struggled to keep back tears. 'I haven't seen him all that time. Mum wouldn't let me. He loved me, my papai . . . He taught me to sail . . . ' her voice trailed off.

'Now I can hardly remember what he looked like. He wouldn't recognize me now.'

'Maybe he would,' I said. 'Maybe you still look much the same as when you were seven, except taller. People don't change that much deep down.'

'I'm going to go and find him,' she said fiercely. 'And Mum can't stop me. No one can. I'm not going to school. I'm going to live with my dad. That's what I'll say, if they come to get me.'

We sailed on. We'd not seen a single boat the whole time. Not heard or seen an aeroplane either. It was like we'd sailed into another world. A dream world. The sun dipped lower in the sky. The clouds disappeared, so now it was completely clear all the way to the horizon. The dark hulk of the islands of St Kilda loomed larger, silhouetted against the sky.

Mara was back at the helm. I was in the bows.

'I can see gannets!' I shouted to her. 'Circling the cliffs! Hundreds of them.'

I tried to remember the other things I'd seen on the St Kilda film. Village Bay, and the rows of stone houses. Soay sheep. Seabirds. Jerky, black and white footage of women in scarves and long dresses scuttling along next to the wall near a jetty, heads down, as if they didn't want their faces to be filmed. They were the last families being taken off the island, in 1930, after two thousand years of people scraping a living off the land and the sea.

'There's some sort of jetty at Village Bay. Let's aim there,' I told Mara. 'Kind of south-east of Hirta, I remember, from the film at school. I think so, anyway.'

Mara nodded.

She'd gone quiet since her outburst about her dad.

'We should eat something,' I said. 'We've not eaten all day. Well, not since lunch.'

Lunch. Mum's crab rolls and a cup of hot chocolate in the tent at the show. It all seemed so long ago, and very far away. What would Mum be doing now? And Fee? Had they noticed I was missing? Was Mum phoning Grandpa and Granny? Calling the air-sea rescue? Was Dad flying over to help search for me? What time was it, even? How long had we been at sea?

'What will your mum do when you don't come home?' I asked Mara. 'Who will she call?'

Mara shrugged. 'She won't notice till it's getting dark.'

'But then what?'

'I don't know. I suppose she'll look to see if *Stardust*'s on the beach. Eventually she'll look in my room. Find the note.'

'What note?'

'Under my pillow.'

'Saying what?'

'I refuse to be sent to that stupid school. And I'm going to live on Heisker. And I want to see my dad. It's my life and I'm in charge of it.'

I imagined Fee, leaving a note like that for Mum. Mum would probably laugh. She wouldn't believe a word of it . . .

But Mara's mum was different. Strange. And Mara was nothing like Fee.

I felt suddenly sorry for Mara. She was so alone. No big family around her, watching out for her, keeping her safe . . .

'Bread and cheese?' I said, rummaging in her bag. 'Apples? More chocolate?'

Mara shook her head. 'You can. I'm not hungry.'

I ate big hunks of bread and cheese. I fed Django some dog biscuits.

The light changed. The sun was low above the water, making a golden pathway all the way to St Kilda. It must be late.

The air got colder.

'Will we get there before it's dark?'

'The sky's clear, it won't get really dark tonight.'

'They'll probably come looking for us soon,' I said. I scanned the sky in all directions, but there was nothing there, not even the vapour trail of a plane on its way to America. Behind us there was no sign of land at all. A damp white mist was creeping over the sea.

'That film . . . It said that sometimes there's a swell,' I said, 'making it hard to land . . . ' I kept racking my brain for more information about St Kilda. I should have paid more attention. 'What is a swell, exactly? Mara?'

She was distracted. Not concentrating. She was shivering.

Something jiggled my mind, something she'd said earlier about the dangers of getting too cold and tired . . .

'Mara! You need a rest. I'll swap for a bit. You need to eat something. Put another jumper on.'

I took over the tiller. I kept an eye on the compass. We were on what Mara called a broad reach, where the wind comes from the side.

The waves slapped under the bows. Were they bigger, now? Darker, too? As if the sea was deeper and colder than before.

We were steadily getting nearer. The sea stacks loomed larger.

'Go about!' Mara suddenly shouted. 'You're going to gybe!'

'What?' I yelled back.

She grabbed the tiller and pushed it way out. The boat shuddered and slowed down as it lost the wind in the sail.

Mara ducked as the boom swung round.

'You've got to keep watching the sail,' she said. 'The wind direction's changing all the time. If you gybe when you don't mean to, you might capsize the boat.'

Capsize?

'You take over,' I said.

'You're doing fine. You're learning fast. Just stay alert. Watch the whole time.' She ate some more cheese. She offered Django some dog biscuits but he wasn't interested.

'Poor Django's still sick,' Mara said. 'He'll be very happy when we land.'

'How long, do you reckon?'

She screwed up her eyes. 'An hour? If we keep up this speed. Maybe a bit more.'

My legs were numb with cold. I pulled the jumper over my knees as best I could with one hand. 'I'll be very happy to land too. You'll sail the last bit into the bay, won't you, Mara? It might be dark by then.'

That word, *capsize,* was still spinning in my brain.

Village Bay

The cliffs of the stacks rose up before us. Huge, more than a thousand feet tall, they blocked out the last rays of the setting sun. It was like sailing towards a mountain. Dark, terrifying walls of cliff, crusted white with the stinking bird poo called *guano*. The smell was enough to make me sick.

And then the boat rocked wildly and we dropped deep down into the trough of a huge wave.

The force threw Mara forward. She grabbed the mast just in time. She yelled my name.

I didn't know what to do. The boat was out of my control. It seemed to rise up, up, up to the top of the crest of the wave. Any minute and we'd crash down again and capsize. I held onto the tiller with all my strength.

Mara scrambled to the stern to help. She loosened my grip on the rope for the mainsail and let it out so it wasn't so tight stretched, but that made it even harder to steer.

Each dip down, down, down was terrible, like we were going down to the bottom of the ocean. Each time it felt like we must surely tip over. We were taking on water. Django slid from one side of the boat to the other until Mara grabbed him and held him tight between her knees. Relentless, one wave and the next and the next took us and pitched us deep down, and then we rose higher and higher, and each time it felt impossible we'd survive.

The sun had long gone. The sky was navy dark, like the sea. We would drown, in darkness, in the terrible ocean, and no one would ever even find our bodies . . .

It seemed to go on like that for hours.

It was nearly dark. The boat crested another wave, slightly smaller than the ones before, and as we dipped and rolled down the other side, through the spume and spray, I glimpsed something other than ocean.

Ahead of us was the curve of a bay, and a sloping beach.

Mara saw it too.

The waves rolling in got smaller.

We limped into the shelter of the bay, the land either side stretched out like arms to protect us from the full force of the sea.

Mara bailed out the water we'd taken on board.

I tightened the sails again. The boat steadied. We could hear each other speak again.

Mara shook her head. 'Extraordinary. I've never been in seas like that.'

'I'm shaking,' I said. 'My legs are like jelly.'

'You were magnificent,' Mara said. 'We're almost there.'

Her words made a warm glow in my belly.

She kept on bailing. I stayed at the helm. And so it was that I, Jamie Robert Mackinnon, sailed *Stardust* into Village Bay, St Kilda.

My finest hour.

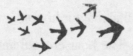

'Those massive waves? That was *swell*,' Mara said. 'Since you asked. Waves that come from a storm hundreds or thousands of miles away. When there's a big empty stretch of ocean with no land in the way they just keep rolling on, uninterrupted. We were lucky not to capsize.'

'Lucky? It was a miracle,' I said.

'Let down both sails. We'll row from here.'

I did what she said on autopilot, too tired to think.

The sails fell in a jumbled heap on the deck. She went forward to untangle the ropes and roll up the sails. I moved to the middle, to untie the oars. My legs ached from sitting for so long: hours of being hunched up, freezing cold and wet and terrified. I could barely feel my fingers.

'The tide's high.' Mara peered through the gloom. 'Is that the jetty? Over there, at the far edge of the bay?'

It was hard to see anything in the dark.

'I'm so cold and wet and tired—' I began.

'Just row,' she said. 'Don't waste energy on moaning.'

The wooden oars hurt my palms. The sail ropes and salt had rubbed the skin into blisters. *I can't do this*, I wanted to say, but I didn't.

Very, slowly, one oar each, we rowed across the bay.

Even at this time of night, white seabirds rose and circled the cliffs. The air stank of fish and old, rank seaweed: the smell of rot and damp and death.

'Stop,' Mara said.

We rested the oars. It was suddenly quiet. Water dripped

from the blades; the boat rocked gently. I heard the wash of water against something solid. I turned and saw the stone hulk of the old jetty, rusted iron rings for mooring, and steps leading down to the water.

We'd made it.

'We'll tie her up here, just for tonight, so we can get on land,' Mara said. 'But she'll smash against the wall if the waves get up. Put the fenders out.'

We stowed the oars under the seats, and fixed the fenders along the side of the boat. Mara went up the steps first, with one bag of stuff, and tied the painter to the mooring ring.

I stood up, picked up the other bag. I stepped from the rocking boat to the solid stone ledge and it felt extraordinary.

But I was shaking all over. Frozen. Too sleepy, almost, to stand.

Mara helped me up the last step onto the jetty.

She waited. She peered down into the boat in the darkness.

'What?' I said.

'Where's Django?' Her voice was full of panic.

'I–I don't know. Django?' I called down.

We waited.

I dumped the bag and went back down the steps.

Even in the dark I could see the boat was empty. There was no sign of him at all.

Mara sobbed. I thought she'd never stop. I was scared I'd start too.

When had I last seen Django? In the swell, he'd definitely still been there: Mara had held onto him to keep him safe.

After that?

Mara called and called his name into the dark.

We listened for an answering bark. We strained our eyes, peering out into the bay. I imagined him paddling to shore, running along the sand, shaking his wet fur . . .

But there was nothing. Only the darkness of an uninhabited island, where there are no lights at all.

The mournful cries of a thousand seabirds . . .

The slap of water against the stone jetty . . .

The suck and draw of waves reaching the shore.

Above us stretched the dark sky, no moon, a scattering of stars.

'Come on,' I said at last. 'We have to find a place to sleep.'

'No,' Mara said. 'I'm going back to look for him.'

'Oh—no—Mara! Not now, in the dark . . . '

'You go on,' she said. 'I'll find you later.'

I didn't even argue. I let her climb back down those steps, untie the rope, set the oars.

I was too tired to think straight. All I wanted was to lie down on land that was dry and didn't rock and sway . . .

and to sleep

and sleep

and sleep.

Lost

I stumbled through the dark, over the rough cobbles of the jetty and onto the island. It was like sleepwalking. I could barely see one step ahead: the darkness was thick like a blanket. And it was as if I was still on the boat, my body rising and falling with the swell. One foot, and then the other. I kept going like that, making myself move one foot at a time, thinking of nothing.

I found a rough path leading uphill, and came to a row of ruined houses.

I dumped the bags and stood in the doorway of the end house. It still had a roof of sorts. I peered into the dense dark. The air smelled rotten and foul: there was no way we could sleep in there. Something moved, and I shrank back in horror.

The thing bleated. A wild sheep or a goat.

I stumbled on, stinging my leg on a load of nettles I hadn't seen in the dark. Maybe we could camp outside tonight. It wasn't raining; there was shelter from the wind against the wall. I rummaged in the bigger bag and found Mara's sleeping bag and the blanket, wrapped them round me.

I was hungry. I ate the rest of the cheese and the bread and then the chocolate.

I thought of Mara rowing across the bay, calling for Django, sad and lonely and exhausted. I tried to listen out for her voice, but all I heard was the sound of the waves breaking onto the shore, and the eerie cries of the seabirds up on the cliff.

I couldn't settle. The ground felt cold and damp. I knew you were supposed to put clothes under you, to keep warm; that you lost heat from your head, too.

Make a fire, I thought. Find something to burn. I staggered down to the shore to search for stuff that had washed up.

The air was cold, coming off the sea, but there seemed to be more light here. The moon was rising, casting silvery patterns on the water. I stared out into the bay, but it was still too dark to see far and there was no sign of Mara or *Stardust* or Django. The waves rushed up the beach, one after another, curling over and breaking, spreading white lace over the sand, and from beyond the bay came the deeper roar of the huge waves battering the sea stacks.

I found bits of driftwood all along the strip of dry sand and pebbles above the tideline, and piled it up. My body ached with tiredness.

I went back one last time to get the blanket and bags. I built a small fire at the top of the beach, spread the blanket out. It was satisfying to light a match and see the dry stuff spark and the flame take hold. Maybe Mara would see the fire from the boat. I added bigger bits of wood, and they steamed and hissed. I began to warm up.

I must have fallen asleep.

Something woke me.

The rhythm of footsteps coming along the sand. For a second I could hardly think where I was or how I'd got there or what was happening.

I opened my eyes. Sat up.

A small, bedraggled figure trudged towards the embers of the fire. Mara.

Alone.

How could it be otherwise? How could a small dog possibly have survived that sea? He must have fallen overboard, struggled, been swamped by the waves . . .

I gulped back tears.

Mara sat down by the fire. She didn't speak.

What could I say? Nothing would make her feel any better.

I fed some more wood into the fire and blew on the glowing embers to make them spark.

'The houses were damp and smelly and horrible. Full of sheep and droppings,' I mumbled. 'It seemed nicer on the beach.'

She nodded. She pulled off her boots. She picked up the sleeping bag and wriggled herself down into it, fully clothed.

We lay either side of the fire. 'Sorry,' I whispered, but she had turned her back to me and I don't think she heard.

I stared at her back. Was she already asleep? Or awake and crying silently for her dog?

Back at home, Mum would be lying awake too, sick with worry. Granny and Grandpa, too, and maybe even Fee. I even imagined Mara's mother, sitting at that table by the window, staring into the darkness. Maybe the whole island knew by now that Mara's boat was missing. That Mara and I had gone too. They'd think we were drowned at sea. Dad would be getting the first flight over in the morning . . .

Sorry.

Sorry.

Sorry.

I got this idea into my head that if I thought hard enough, I could somehow send the message to Mum that I was OK. That she would sense it. Like telepathy. I focused my whole mind on thinking the words to her. *I'm alive. I'm OK. Don't worry, Mum.* I sent my message over and over.

And then I thought of a small dog, paddling bravely towards shore, trying to hold his head up, struggling to breathe.

Don't give up.

Morning

When I next woke, it was the grey light of dawn. I was cold. The air was damp. Our fire had died to ash.

Mara had turned in the night towards the fire: her hair lay in damp strands over her cheek. Her eyes were shut. Dirty tear marks stained her face. I watched her breath rise and fall as she slept.

The sea was quiet. No wind. The seabirds circled the cliffs, shrieking and calling their wild cries.

I went to collect more wood for the fire.

All along the tideline the sea had dumped debris—tangled kelp, strands of seaweed, plastic bottles, shells and bits of rope. I moved along cautiously, afraid of what else I might find washed up.

Ahead of me, the retreating tide left a small bundle of some-thing on the wet sand. My heart lurched. Please, let it not be . . . I couldn't bear to be the one to find him . . .

Phew. Already I could see it was just a heap of brown seaweed. I walked on.

I found a wooden crate that would be good for the fire once it dried out. I stacked the crate at the top of the beach with the other bits of wood I'd collected last night.

Mara still slept.

I ran the length of the beach to warm up. In the early morning light, the island seemed different—less spooky and menacing.

I scrambled up the steep slope behind the ruined houses, and there was the sun rising, glowing gold above the sea. I turned my face to feel its warmth, closed my eyes against the brightness.

I climbed higher.

The next time I stopped, the air was full of the cries of seabirds—fulmars and kittiwakes, gannets. I watched them circle and dive till my head reeled too.

Higher still, I flopped onto the grass to catch my breath. Different birds called. A wren whistled. A skylark spiralled up, weaving its column of song. I rested on my elbows and stared out to sea. Mist hung in layers all the way to the horizon. The nearest sea stack wore a halo of cloud. There was no sign of a rescue helicopter or lifeboat. Why would there be? No one would ever imagine we'd sail all this way and survive.

On I went, clambering up the steep slope. My legs ached but I pushed myself further. I wanted to stand at the very top, and look out over that massive ocean stretching uninterrupted all the way to America. Newfoundland.

I startled a clutch of wild sheep that had been sleeping in a ruined stone sheepfold. They ran, scattering across the hillside, bleating with fear. Perhaps they'd not seen a person for a very long time. I thought of the photos in Grandpa's book. A hundred years ago, the islanders kept sheep for their wool, wove and knitted it into strange lumpy garments and blankets. Perhaps these sheep were their descendants, gone wild.

At last I puffed up the final rocky outcrop.

And there was my view!

Green-blue sea. Sky. Nothing else. I stretched out my arms and let the wind buffet me.

Me. Standing on the edge of the world.

This side of the hill was in deep shadow. The ground went in a series of rocky steps down to a grassy ledge, and then it was crumbling, rocky cliff. There were fewer seabirds—I guessed this side of the island was blasted and battered by storms—but a pair of great skuas were kicking up a fuss, diving and trying to drive something off the ledge.

Another bird?

A sheep?

A fox?

I peered down into the gloom. The air was dank and cold. The sea churned and frothed at the foot of the cliff. For a second I felt dizzy and sick.

It took me a while to work out what I was seeing. My brain told me it was impossible. I stared until my eyes watered. I blinked, and it was still there.

The angry birds were attacking a small brown dog.

Django?

I yelled. My voice was swept away on the wind, drowned by the roar of water. I threw a pebble to scare away the birds. It bounced and ricocheted off the rocks, tumbled further down— and fell short. And what if I hit Django instead, by mistake? I didn't try again.

But it was enough to unnerve the birds. And that gave him a chance to breathe, and he looked up, and he must have seen me because he barked, and yipped, as if he had a sudden surge of new energy. Even from so high up, I could tell his tail was wagging wildly.

The birds drew off, startled. They banked away, swerved off.

Somehow, Django had survived the sea. He had swum or been swept by tide and currents onto the island, spat out onto the rocks, and climbed his way to a safe ledge.

I called his name. I clambered slowly down the rocks, trying not to look at the drop below. Each time my feet slithered and slipped on loose stones my heart lurched.

His paws were obviously sore, and he looked half dead, but Django started climbing up to meet me. He stopped, and whined, and shook his still-damp fur.

I finally reached him. 'Django!' I hugged him close.

I told him how happy I was he was safe. I told him Mara would be the happiest person on the planet. I held him tight.

He wagged his tail, he licked my face. He whimpered and cried like a baby.

It took me ages to climb back, holding Django under one arm and using the other hand to clutch on to clumps of grass and rock to pull myself up.

We finally got back to Village Bay. Django seemed to get heavier with each step. But we were nearly there. I could see Mara by the fire.

Django saw her too. He scrabbled out of my arms. He ran to her on his sore paws. He wagged his tail and threw himself on her. He yelped and whined and licked her face.

Mara sobbed.

Her face shone at the wonder of it all.

She wanted me to tell her the story of finding him, over and over again.

'What do you think happened?' she said.

'He must have fallen overboard when we were coming into the bay, and had to swim, and the sea washed him up on the other side of the headland,' I said. 'And he climbed up the cliff, slowly. All night, it took him. Perhaps he knew you were on the island too, and was coming to look for you. Dogs know all sorts.'

Mara hugged him. She wept into his fur. She wouldn't let him go.

She and Django dozed together in the warmth of the fire. The early morning sunshine got stronger as the sun rose higher. Everything seemed at peace.

I sat by the fire and fed it pieces of wood each time it burned too low. I was hungry, and we had hardly anything left to eat. I thought again about my family, waking up to No News.

Today I'd have to work on Mara, show her how we couldn't possibly stay.

The sun rose higher. The seabirds got noisier.

Perhaps the rescue helicopter would come later today. The lifeboat might appear any moment.

Why hadn't they come searching already?

Because they thought we'd gone to the fishing islands and drowned, that's why. They'd be searching the wrong bit of sea.

Mara woke up properly. 'Good morning!' she said, and stretched. She wriggled in the sleeping bag closer to the fire and warmed her face. She looked totally different. Happy, strong. The old Mara was back again.

Django shook out his fur. He looked better too.

'I need a pee and a wash!' Mara announced. 'Then break-fast.' She wriggled out of the sleeping bag and ran up the beach towards the grass field and the ruined houses.

I rummaged through the bags to see what food was left. I found an actual frying pan, and a bowl and spoon, two damp slices of stale bread, and a tin of beans and sausage. No tin opener. I used a knife to stab my way in. I emptied the tin into the frying pan and balanced that over the fire.

Mara came back. She looked totally relaxed, as if this was what she'd wanted all along. 'Great,' she said. 'Breakfast. Then we can explore and make a proper shelter. One of the houses has most of its roof but it smells rank. We can clean it out.'

She was excited about everything.

I went along with it.

We ate everything and it was the best breakfast ever. Mara gave Django the frying pan to lick out. She poured some fresh-water into it afterwards, and he lapped it up. 'His paws are sore,' she said. 'He needs to rest today.'

We washed up the bowl and the pan in the sea.

I sat on the rocks.

Mara went along the tideline, collecting shells and pieces of sea glass, and bits and bobs like string and fishing net that might be useful.

Django lay by the fire, licking his paws, watching Mara like a hawk, but too sore and tired to follow her along the beach.

The wind picked up. The waves became white horses, galloping into the bay. I still expected a boat to come around the headland any moment, or the rescue helicopter to whirr into view.

Ghosts

The roar of the waves beyond Village Bay got louder. Another huge swell must be coming in off the Atlantic. I thought of the thousands of miles of open water between here and America. What if we hadn't landed here, last night?

Even in the shelter of the bay, the waves were rough, now, steadily rolling in. White surf crashed and pounded the beach. There was no way we'd be able to get off the island today, even if I could persuade Mara.

No one could arrive by boat.

There'd be no rescue today.

Did I want to be rescued? That was the weirdest thing. I wanted Mum and Dad to know I was alive. But I wanted to explore the island, to make fires and cook fish and have a proper real adventure, too. And I wanted Mara to know I was on her side. I did care about her.

Where was she?

The beach was empty. Django must have gone with her.

I went in and out of the ruined houses, looking for Mara.

One house was much less smelly and damp than the others, so I went right in. This must be the one she'd found earlier.

It was dark inside, what with the low roof and tiny windows. My eyes adjusted to the gloom, and I saw more stuff—a table, a chair, the remains of a fireplace; even pots and pans, rusty and ancient, on a shelf, and the shredded remains of an old piece of cloth. Everything smelled musty.

I went to the doorway to check the boat was still tied up safe at the jetty. It rocked and tugged on its mooring, bashing against the stone jetty as the tide rose.

Still no sign of Mara.

I wiped the cobwebs off the chair with my sleeve and sat down. I listened to the wind and the seabirds. This is what the children who lived here would have heard. I tried to imagine their lives. They had a school and a church and they'd have worked hard on the land, growing food, made their own clothes and told stories. They'd have been happy and sad and scared and excited just the same as us.

Perhaps they'd left other things behind. What would I have done, if I'd had to leave my home and my island? Would I have left a message, or a special object like a knife or a photo or something . . .

It was strange. I began to imagine I heard actual voices, speaking—and then I heard footsteps. Someone was standing in the doorway, silhouetted against the light.

'Made you jump!' Mara laughed. 'Thought I was a ghost girl, didn't you?'

'Course not.'

'And this is the ghost dog.' She put Django down on the floor. He shivered and whined as if he could smell real ghosts in the house.

'Where did you go?' I said. 'You disappeared.'

'I went exploring. And guess what? There's a load of army huts, and a massive communications mast and satellite thing, and a house. A proper house.'

'Someone lives here?' My heart beat wildly. This was it! Finally I could send a message to Mum and Grandpa.

'It's for a warden. But they aren't here, luckily. It's all shut up. There's a sign on a noticeboard saying you have to drop anchor in the bay not tie up at the jetty, and another one about NO DOGS allowed 'cause of the rare birds that nest here.' She laughed. 'And I found a well, and a graveyard.' She was very pleased with herself.

I was thinking about the warden who could have been here. But wasn't.

'Want to see?' Mara said.

I followed her outside. The wind was blowing strong. The sea boomed and pounded beyond the bay.

We examined the army sheds. The doors were padlocked. We peered through the windows. Old-fashioned furniture was piled up: a trestle table, metal chairs with canvas backs and seats. Boxes. Everything was covered in furry dust and spider webs. No one had been here for a long time. The ugly fuel tanks with *Danger* signs plastered over them looked disused, rusty. Perhaps all the military stuff was left over from the war ages ago.

'They might have used this island for missile practice,' I said. 'There might be unexploded shells. We should be careful.'

'You're always too careful,' Mara said. 'Though you're getting better.'

'What do you mean?'

'You were scared of everything when I first met you,' Mara said.

'Like what?'

'The sea. Swimming. Sailing. But not any more. You've got braver.'

She was right, but I wasn't going to tell her that. Or that it was because of her.

'Want to see the warden's house now?' She led the way, past the last ruined house and beyond the end of the jetty.

That must be why we'd missed seeing it last night, in the dark.

It had whitewashed walls and a proper roof and solid wooden door, painted green. We opened the gate and went right up to the door. We tried to peer into the windows through the gaps between the boards. No chance.

'It's all boarded up for winter.'

'Imagine winter here! The winds and the storms and the rain lashing the island; the long dark days and nights! Exciting!' Mara said.

Cold. Wet. Dark. Lonely. Miserable. I didn't say that to Mara, though. I wasn't going to give her more ammunition against me.

We clambered up the rocks the other side of the jetty. This time, I went first.

I gulped.

I was on the edge of a cliff, with a massive drop straight down to churning sea. I stepped back quickly, my heart thumping wildly.

I climbed back down. My legs were shaking.

It was easy to see why the people of St Kilda had lived along Village Bay. It was the only flattish bit of the island: a small apron of field between massive cliffs. We scrambled up the hill above the village, so I could show Mara the place where I'd found Django.

'Let's sit down,' Mara said. 'Django's getting too heavy to carry any further.'

We sat down on a pile of stones, remains of an old shelter or sheep fold. Django sat between us.

I stroked his head and his velvet ears.

'People were born and lived and died here for hundreds and thousands of years,' Mara said. 'They grew their food and looked after their animals, lived their whole lives here, happy enough.'

I looked northwards, out over the grey-blue sea to the sea

stacks, and the other islands, steeper even than this one. Beyond that, in every direction, there was nothing but ocean, ocean, ocean.

Somewhere to the south east, lost in the mist and the cloud, was home.

'I know you want to go back,' Mara said. 'I know you're worried about your mum and dad.'

I didn't say anything.

'We can't go today. It's much too rough. So let's just enjoy being here. Tomorrow, or the next day, we can sail back.'

'If only we could get them a message, it would be different,' I said.

Mara nodded. She pulled her jumper over her knees. Her hair blew around her face.

We sat without speaking, each lost in our own thoughts.

Mara got up. She picked up Django. 'Come on. Let's go back down and get the fishing stuff from the boat and start catching our dinner.'

Wind and Stars

All afternoon, we fished off the rocks. We caught seven silver mackerel. We collected wood—bits of broken chair leg and other stuff from the ruined houses, because the new driftwood on the beach was still too wet to burn—and made a fire to cook them on.

'You scrape the silver scales off the skin first, remember,' Mara said. 'Then slice down the fish belly and scoop out the guts.' She took a knife from the box and showed me how. The gulls grabbed the bloody raw mess she threw onto the water. 'Disgusting things.'

We cooked the fish in the frying pan balanced at the edge of the fire. I had never tasted anything so delicious.

Three fish each and we were both stuffed. We gave the last fish to Django. He wolfed it down, bones and all.

I put more wood onto the fire: bits of broken chair, and the pallet that had dried out in the wind. We sat either side of the fire and held our faces towards the warmth of the flames and when we got too hot we sat the other way, to warm our backs. We drank water from the bottles Mara had brought: the salty fish made us thirsty.

The light faded. The wind dropped.

'Tell me more about your dad,' I said.

'He was funny,' Mara said. 'He made up silly songs and stories. He got angry sometimes. Not with me, but with Mum.' She thought for a while. 'It's getting harder to remember,' she said quietly.

'He never had much money. He was a fisherman, like his papai before him. The house was full of fishing nets and stuff and it was cold in the winter, because there were gaps round the windows and only one stove, in the living room.'

I thought of Mara's island home, not much more than a fisherman's shack.

'But he had lots of friends. Too many, Mum said.' Mara poked the fire to make sparks fly up. 'Drinking and singing and laughing and having a good time.'

'What's wrong with that?' I asked.

Mara shrugged. 'Nothing. I don't know.' She sounded suddenly uneasy. 'But Mum didn't like it.'

I thought of her mum, without any friends at all.

'And didn't your dad want you to go to school?'

Mara thought for a while.

'He showed me how to fish and he showed me how to sail and he encouraged me to sing and dance. And that was enough.

'I was only little,' she said.

The wet rocks shone in a brief gleam of evening sunlight. Most of the beach was in deep shadow.

Mara sang an old song.

'I'm just a poor wayfaring stranger
Travelling through this world of woe . . . '

'Sing something happy,' I told her.

'The best songs are all sad,' she said.

'Why?'

'I dunno. It's just the way it is. I'll make up a happy one, if you like.' She hummed and danced along the beach away from me, to practise.

Django stayed by the fire next to me but he watched her the whole time as if he'd never let her out of his sight ever again.

Mara looked perfectly at home, like she always did on a beach. She skipped along the sand, crouched down to pick up shells, danced further away. She sang her made-up happy song. Fragments drifted over to me.

'The wind the stars the sparkling sea
They fill my heart and set me free . . . '

I rummaged in the bag just in case there was any chocolate left. I found dog biscuits, and a packet of oatcakes, a bruised apple.

'I dance and run and clap my hands
My feet leave footprints on the sand
We won't go back where troubles are
We love this place of wind and star.'

I found something else—a book, I thought at first, but when I opened it I saw it was full of drawings, scribbled words. Pencil sketches of boats, and seals, and birds; pictures of shells and the curve of a bay.

Mara snatched the notebook out of my hands. 'Oi! You shouldn't look at other people's things.' She'd danced back without me noticing.

'Did you do the drawings?'

She hugged the book to her. 'It's private. Not for you to see.'

'Sorry,' I said. 'But they are really good. I didn't know you could draw.'

I could tell she was pleased, whatever she pretended.

'Did you bring pens and stuff, too? We could write a message and put it in a bottle and it will wash up somewhere the other side of the world.'

She liked that idea.

She scrabbled in the bag and brought out a tin of coloured pencils. She tore out a page from the notebook. 'You do the writing.'

'What shall I put?'

'You decide.' She drew a picture of *Stardust* with me and her and Django on board, waving. She shaded in the sea, and the sky.

I watched her. 'Brilliant,' I said. 'You should show those

schools' people your notebook. That would show them what you can do, without you even having a teacher.'

She passed the page to me. 'Now you write some words.'

I thought hard.

Hello from Mara, Jamie and a dog called Django. We are having an adventure on St Kilda, the last island between Scotland and America. We sailed here by ourselves on the good ship Stardust.

'Read it out aloud,' Mara said. 'Your handwriting is too spidery.' She peered over my shoulder as I read out the words.

'OK?'

She nodded.

I rolled up the paper. 'Now we need a bottle.' I drank the last mouthfuls of water from one of Mara's plastic bottles, and put the rolled up note inside.

We climbed the slippery rocks at the edge of the bay, and Mara threw the bottle as far as she could. We watched it bob out to sea, dipping and rocking over the waves as the tide took it out. We watched it until our eyes ached and we couldn't see it any more.

A great wash of sadness came over me. I imagined Mum

sitting at the kitchen table with her head in her hands, mad with worry and grief. I imagined Fee frantically searching the internet for news, swearing each time the connection went down. I imagined Dad, flying back to the island; Grandpa, dragging the *Kathleen Mary* out of the shed and launching it at the harbour, sailing off to try to find us . . .

'Tomorrow we definitely have to sail back,' I told Mara. 'It's not right, us being here. Our parents will think we're dead and drowned. We mustn't stay any longer, however fun it is.'

Mara turned away and sang her made-up happy song over and over, and I knew she did not want to think about leaving. Or, more likely, about what she had to face when she got back.

'I understand what it's like,' I said.

'What's like?'

'Not wanting to go to school.'

'Do you?'

'And missing your dad. I miss mine, and I get to see him every few weeks. It must be terrible for you.'

She sat scrunched up, her face away from the light. I could hear the tightness in her voice. She was trying not to show how upset she was. I knew what that was like, too.

'I hated my old school,' I said. 'That's one reason why we moved, 'cause I was so miserable.' I told her a bit about the tests, and the bullies, and my sarcastic teacher. The way everything was a competition with winners. Losers. About me not having a proper friend. 'There was no one like me,' I said.

She listened intently.

'We can tell my mum about it all,' I said. 'She could talk to your mum. Maybe we can help find your dad for you. You don't have to do everything by yourself, Mara.'

She was quiet for a long, long time. But her shoulders were shaking, so I knew she was crying. I didn't do anything but stay there, near her, and it seemed that was enough to make a difference.

We decided to sleep on the beach by the fire again—we agreed it was too creepy in the house. There were too many spiders. It smelled too old.

We drank the last of the water Mara had brought.

'That's another good reason we have to go tomorrow,' I said. 'Water is the one thing you must have to survive. You can go without food for ages, but not without fresh water.'

'There's the well,' Mara said. 'We could drink water from that.'

'No way! It's probably swarming with bugs. We'd get sick.'

'OK,' Mara said. 'But I bet the warden drinks it in the summer. Where else could the water come from for the house?'

'So,' I said. 'That's settled. We leave tomorrow.'

But what if the weather was too stormy? The tide and current wrong? A massive swell coming in?

What then? My mind whirled with worry.

We lay close to the fire. It burned lower until it was nothing but glowing embers.

Mara crawled into the sleeping bag.

I pulled up the blanket over me. Django crept under the blanket too, and his warm body was comforting.

I lay on my back and stared at the sky.

So many stars. A whole wide firmament of glittering stars: a trillion cold eyes staring back down at us.

The world seemed enormous.

So much space.

Unimaginable distances.

Engine

Django woke me. He sat bolt upright, as if he'd heard something. The hairs along his spine bristled.

I listened.

The seabirds shrieked and cried, circling the cliffs. Was there another sound? The low *thrum* of an engine? Or was I imagining it?

I scrabbled up on to my feet. I scanned the sky. It was that early morning light, before the sun is properly up and everything looks amazing: new and hopeful. The sky was a pale blue, empty as far as the horizon. Mist lay in layers over the sea. No sign of anything like a rescue plane as far as I could see.

Mara was still asleep.

'Lie down,' I told Django. 'Stay here.'

He settled back down next to Mara.

I climbed up onto the grass above the beach, ran through the gap between the houses and climbed the hill behind to get a bigger view. I should have brought something white or shiny to wave. What if there was a plane and it missed us?

I climbed higher.

I scanned the sky to the horizon, but the sky was empty.

Had I imagined the sound?

There. Now I saw, or thought I saw, a tiny dot on the sea that wasn't a rock, that seemed to be moving.

North-east, way beyond the tiny island of Boreray: a boat.

My heart beat faster. The boat must have an engine, so a lobster fishing boat, perhaps, or a rescue RIB. Sound travels very long distances over water in the clear air.

The mist lifted and for a moment the island was flooded with golden light.

I sat and watched.

I was sure it was a boat, though it was hard to see it clearly, silhouetted against the sun. It faltered, changed course slightly as the wind shifted.

The mist over the water thinned.

Now I could see it wasn't a lifeboat, or anything remotely like a rescue boat.

It had brown sails, gaff-rigged, like the traditional fishing boats, a bit like the ones Grandpa built and restored—*Never Broken in a Sea*—except bigger, with an engine or outboard.

Could it be?

Or was I imagining the whole thing, conjuring it in my own mind because I so wanted it to be true?

My eyes watered from so much staring.

It was a calm sea, perfect sailing weather, a light wind and the smallest waves.

The boat was heading on full sail towards Boreray. In less than two hours it could be sailing into Village Bay. For a wild moment I imagined it was actually Grandpa, sailing out to find us, following some instinct that he would find us here . . .

I ran down the hill to tell Mara.

I stopped once, where the land dipped in the grassy valley, to catch my breath and press my hand against the stitch in my side. I couldn't see Mara or the beach from here.

How would she react?

I came up over the side of the dip and saw the sweep of the bay. Mara was packing up the bags. She stamped out the last embers of the fire.

I waved and yelled and she waved back.

'There's a boat!' I called. 'It's coming this way.'

'I know,' Mara called back. 'Time to go. Hurry up!'

For a second I was speechless.

'No, No!' I shouted. 'Wait, Mara! Listen to me!'

I caught her up. I begged and pleaded with her. 'It's a fishing boat. It will have radio and satellite on board. We can let our families know we're OK. Please, Mara. You've made your point, now. Your mum and everyone will listen to what you say. I'll help you. Everyone will. Honestly, Mara.'

She was already walking away from me. I pulled her back. 'Listen to me. We've got no food or water. We can't sail that distance.'

She tugged away. 'What distance?'

'Back. There's nowhere else to go. This is the last island. Mara!'

'We can leave a message to say we're safe,' Mara said. 'Or you can stay and tell them and be rescued if you want. Fair enough. Your choice, Jamie. You're a free person. And so am I. That's my point. If I'm going back, I'm going in my boat, under my own sails, 'cause I choose to.'

I knew I shouldn't let Mara go alone. And I couldn't make her stay. I tried and tried.

Mara dug deep in the dry bag, and handed me a pencil. She tore a page from her notebook. We wrote a letter. We pinned it to the noticeboard with the rusted drawing pins from the warden's notice about nesting birds.

Hello. This is Mara and Jamie. We are safe. We are sorry for the trouble we have caused and for making you worry so much. (I insisted we write that). Please contact Mrs Kathleen Mackinnon on this number (07893 112345) to tell her we are fine.

We sailed and camped here on the last island as Mara's protest to make the Island's Education Authority and Mara's Mum understand that Mara refuses to be sent away to school. She demands her right to see her dad. We are sailing back home in Stardust now and we are fine and do not need rescuing.

Mara is responsible for this decision and it is not Jamie's fault.

(She insisted we write that).

We signed our names at the bottom.

'We should add today's date,' I said. 'In case that fishing boat doesn't land here after all.'

We had to work it out. It seemed absolutely ages since we left, but it was only three days.

Saturday August 21st

'The tide's turning. It's the perfect time to be sailing,' Mara said. She stuffed the bags under the seats and tied them on. She tied Django, too, this time. He flumped to the deck with his head between his paws, resigned to misery at sea. We buckled our life jackets, still damp from the journey here.

I untied the rope and we slipped the mooring. We rowed easily out into Village Bay, helped by the tide. As soon as we were far enough out to catch the breeze, we set the sails. Mara took the tiller and I went forward to check the depth. I let the centreboard down fully and pulled the foresail tight.

'Ready? Brace yourself,' Mara yelled, as we got to the end of the sheltered bay and met the open ocean.

Live Your Life

Django trembled and cowered under the wooden slats of the seat, and pressed against my leg. His body seemed smaller, thinner than before. Out here, it was freezing.

'It's OK, boy,' I told him. 'We're heading home.' He lifted his head as if he recognized that word. 'Home!' I said again, and his tail thumped.

Mara sang as she steered the boat, but the wind snatched the song and threw it skywards and I couldn't make out the words.

A sad song, or a happy one?

How small and fragile a boat seems, when you're out in the middle of an ocean. It seemed extraordinary that such a tiny boat could stay afloat, and keep us safe.

Not dry, though. The biggest waves washed over the edge and even the small ones threw up a fine salty spray. I kept baling, and even so my feet squelched in inches of water at the bottom of the boat.

Could we survive the swell a second time?

But I needn't have worried: the waves were much smaller this time, and the tide and the wind were with us. The boat sailed smoothly along, the water washing under the bows as we rode the waves. Up up up . . . and deep down, as the waves rolled out.

The first bout of seasickness came and went.

We began to be hungry instead. We ate the oatcakes, but they were dry and scratchy on our throats and we had nothing to drink.

'How many hours till we get back?'

'Ten? Twelve?'

How long had it taken us to come this far, before? I tried to remember.

'I'll take over when you need a rest,' I called to Mara, and she nodded.

I checked behind us for the fishing boat but there was no sign of it. Perhaps we'd missed the moment it came round into the bay. Or perhaps it had simply gone further out to drop lobster pots near the sea stacks and had no idea about us at all.

Sunlight patterned the waves. Gulls circled the boat; further off, huge white birds with black-tipped wings dived for fish. Gannets. A second flock of puffins swam low across the water in front of the boat.

'Isn't it beautiful?' Mara shouted above the wind. 'Doesn't it make you happy?'

'Yes!' I shouted back, and that was the truth, that moment. We seemed to be flying through the waves now, borne by the tide and the current and the steady westerly wind in the sails.

Mara sang a new made-up happy song, really loud. She laughed. 'Join in.'

'I'm rubbish at singing.'

'Stop saying you're rubbish at things. Just do it!'

'*Wind in my hair, wind in the sail, wind in Django's tail!*' I yelled along with her. Her silly song made me laugh, too.

'*We're zipping along on a fast running tide and now there's no need to . . .* ' She cast about for a word that might rhyme. 'Fail? Bail?'

'And we'll live to tell the tale!'

'If we're lucky we'll see a whale!'

We made up lines and yelled them at the tops of our voices.

I slid along the seat closer to Mara so we could talk more easily.

'What's going to happen when we get back?'

'What do you mean?'

'Everyone will be furious. All the worry about us, and the rescue people's time and expense and everything.'

Mara sighed. 'It's kind-of the point. To make my mum listen to me, and what I need. To show the schools' people I'm deadly serious about not going.

'My mother's not like yours, Jamie. Not that I know your mum, but I can tell by how you are and things you say.

'My mum's in a world of her own, mostly. She lives in her head. She doesn't think about me.'

'So, wouldn't it be better for you to be away at school?' I said.

Mara didn't answer. She was studying the compass, adjusting direction, totally focused on sailing the boat safely home.

I started making plans in my head. Perhaps Mara could come and live with us. Perhaps we could help her find her dad and visit him. Could she do some days at my school, just to try it? She might discover she liked it after all.

We seemed to have been sailing for hours but we'd no real way of knowing exactly how long, except by the arc of the sun, moving slowly westwards. It was behind us, now.

'I'm sleepy,' I said. 'It's all the same, just sea and more sea. How do people manage to sail really long distances, like across the Atlantic? How come they don't get bored?'

'They do, probably,' Mara said. 'If you were on a long distance, you'd have a bigger boat and a cooker and cabin and stuff. You could set a course and then get on with other things like making dinner, as long as you kept an eye out for other ships. But you can travel thousands of miles and hardly see a single other boat. One day, that's what I'm going to do.'

'Really?'

She nodded. 'Yes. A big, amazing, adventurous voyage. Sail across the Atlantic and then through the Panama Canal and across the Pacific. Find an island of my own. Live there.'

I laughed. 'You probably actually will, knowing you.'

'And why not? I want to live a big life, full of new things and new experiences. I'm going to find a way to live that makes me happy.'

I nodded. I believed she would.

I'd never met anyone like Mara. I'd never heard anyone talk like that about their future. It was like she opened up a door or a window in my own head. I too could do anything. I might not be as bold and wild and crazy as Mara, but I could still do something amazing with my life, like her.

Something Out There

The light changed again; behind us, the sun burned low in the sky and the wake from our boat was touched with flecks of gold.

'I think I can see land,' I shouted to Mara.

The low line of grey on the horizon was our first glimpse of the fishing islands. Three low islands. The biggest was Heisker. And that meant we were on course, and that soon we'd be getting to the reef, and then we'd be nearly home.

Was it simply the light playing tricks or was there something else out there? Small, but not rocks or a bird.

'Look ahead,' I said to Mara. 'Slightly to the right–'

'Starboard, you mean.'

'Yes. It's not just the waves, and it's definitely bigger than a bird. Moving . . . ' I squinted to try and focus.

Not a rescue boat. Not a dinghy or rowing boat.

Mara kept a steady course, one hand on the tiller adjusting our direction ever so slightly. The boat lifted and dropped with each rolling wave.

'It's dolphins!' I yelled.

'Yay!' Mara whooped.

The first one breached the waves followed by a second, and third, and more . . . leaping and disappearing again under the water. They swam even closer.

They swam under the boat, beside the boat, they leapt in the wake we left behind and they dived under the bows. I went forward and crept along the deck so I was close up enough to see their blue-grey skin and bright strange eyes and hear the click of their voices as they cavorted in the bow wave.

'They're playing!' I shouted to Mara. 'They're having fun!'

For maybe fifteen or twenty magical minutes the dolphins accompanied us as we sailed towards Heisker, and then, as suddenly as they had arrived, they left.

Mara's face shone with happiness.

For a few minutes, neither of us could speak.

'Joyful,' Mara said. That's what they were. Wild. Free. One day, I shall swim with dolphins.'

'It'd have to be warmer sea, then,' I said.

'It will be. West Africa: Atlantic coast. Or the Cabo Verde islands.'

'How do you *know* this stuff?' I said.

'I like maps,' Mara said. 'Maps and charts and my World Atlas.'

'Me too.' I thought about the map of our island, spread out on the kitchen table, and Mum telling me to clear it away ready for supper. I'd die for supper right that minute. Not *literally* die; that would be stupid . . .

'Shall we try and find the harbour entrance on Heisker?' Mara said, as we sailed closer. 'Camp out one more night?'

I glanced at her. She was joking, right?

She grinned. Yes, she was.

The distant roar grew louder.

'Hear that?' Mara said. 'It's the surf on the reef.'

'Does it sound good or bad?'

'Can't tell yet. Even on a calm day it sounds loud. The important thing is the state of the tide. It was on the turn at Village Bay, ebbing, but that was hours and hours ago.'

'What would be best?'

'A rising tide. Going in. With luck, we might sweep through on a wave like we did before.'

I peered ahead. It was getting dark. The line of white surf ahead glowed in the light from the setting sun.

'It's too late to worry now,' Mara said. 'We just have to do it.' She sounded tired.

'Shall I take over for a bit?'

She nodded. We swapped places.

I checked the compass position, adjusted the tiller ever so slightly to keep the wind in the sail.

Mara sat beside Django. She rubbed his damp body to warm him up.

We'd made really good progress. There was still just a little light in the sky.

'What's that?' Mara said.

'What?'

'That sound. Not the surf, something else.'

We strained to listen above the roar of the surf and the rhythmic smack of water under the bows.

'Is there a boat?'

We looked at each other. Were we about to be rescued?

When we didn't need to be rescued?

Out of the low bank of cloud in the far distance, over where the island archipelago must be, came a helicopter.

The whirring sound got louder until it filled our heads and drowned all thoughts and made it impossible to hear each other speak.

A massive beam of light shone on the water, blindingly bright.

Air-Sea Rescue

The downdraught from the helicopter blades whipped up the waves around us. They'd capsize us if they came much lower. No way could they rescue us from the air.

Mara grabbed the tiller from me. She tried to steer us away into calmer sea.

The helicopter hovered. It came low enough for me to see the open door and a guy in a yellow helmet and safety harness looking down at us. He waved and called out something, but we couldn't hear much above the whirr of the blades. I guessed he was asking if we were OK.

'Wave back,' Mara shouted. 'Show him we're totally fine. And make him go away.'

I waved at the guy, did the thumbs-up thing with both thumbs, tried to show him that the helicopter was making the waves rough.

He understood. He thumbs-upped back and spoke into a radio transmitter. He waved again. He mouthed something. *Lifeboat?*

The helicopter tipped and swerved away. The whirring sound faded into the distance.

It was the weirdest thing, to have actually seen someone else after so long on our own. And now they'd gone again. We were still on our own.

'He'll be reporting back to say we're OK.' I thought of Mum. Dad. Grandpa.

'No way could he have rescued us anyway. No way he could winch down on to *Stardust*! They'll probably call out the life-boat.

'Not that we need rescuing,' I added, but I needn't have bothered: Mara couldn't hear a word I was saying above the pounding surf.

We were almost at the reef. But the light was fading fast; it was much harder to see the gap we'd come through before.

'I think we're OK,' she yelled. 'I think the tide's pulling us in, and the fact we can see the rocks means it's not high tide yet.'

I went forward. I hooked one arm tight round the mast to keep me stable.

Django whimpered. He sniffed the air, as if he sensed landfall.

'We're too far to the left,' I yelled. 'Steer right, Mara. Starboard.'

She nodded.

The boat rocked as the waves rolled under us. Each one took us forward in a lurch, and the waves seemed to build and build as they approached the reef, crashing in foaming white water as they smashed onto them. But there was one place where the water stayed black: that must be our gap.

Mara saw it too.

She slackened the rope to let some of the wind out of the mainsail, she steered to starboard. 'Hold on!' she screamed as another wave came from behind and lifted us up and up, and then we were riding the surf itself, and the rocks loomed up on either side.

I glanced back at Mara: her wild hair blowing around her face, her mouth set firm like she'd do this or die.

A wave washed over the bows and drenched me. I spluttered

and choked. For a second I felt myself slip, but I caught the handhold just in time as the boat lurched again.

The next wave swept us through the gap.

Water streamed down my face. Salt tears mixed with sea spray.

Mara whooped and yelled, triumphant.

I punched the air.

We were nearly home at last. Not dead and drowned after all.

It was as if going through the reefs had taken every last ounce of Mara's energy. She had nothing left. I didn't notice at first; it wasn't until the sail started to flap that I realized she'd stopped checking the compass and we were going off course.

I edged back along the boat and sat next to her.

'Mara?' I took the tiller and she hardly seemed to notice. Her hands were freezing. 'Are you ill?'

She seemed to be slipping into sleep. She didn't answer me.

I started to panic. I should warm her up. Get that blanket from the bag. Find something for her to eat. But I couldn't do that at the same time as steer the boat. And there was no food.

I reassured myself: we'd been seen. A lifeboat would come any minute.

I kept talking to her. I said things I wouldn't have said normally. But none of this was normal. I told her she was amazing. The best friend. That she'd changed me. I'd learned so many things from her. She was totally brilliant. Braver and bolder and cleverer and wilder than anyone else I knew.

'We're nearly there,' I said over and over.

How was I going to land the boat? I'd not done that before. I didn't know how to find the beach where her house was, even. Should I take down the sails and row in? How could I do all that at the same time as keep the boat steady and not capsize in the waves? My head whirred and spun and I couldn't work anything out any more. Was I getting ill too? I was more and more muddled.

I peered into the darkness. The slow drawn-out fading of the light had tipped into pitch black without me realizing. There was no moon, no stars. Low cloud had swept in. I felt the first spits of rain.

The wind changed too. It gusted, and each gust tipped the boat and made everything judder. I tried to remember what Mara had taught me about reefing the sails in a strong wind.

How far was land?

Were those lights ahead?

Not lights from the land, though. Not the sweep of a lighthouse beam or the bright helicopter searchlights, either, or the strong light of a lifeboat. These were the small winking lights, red and green for port and starboard, on a sailing dinghy.

I shook Mara's arm. 'There's a boat. Someone's coming to help. Wake up, Mara. It's going to be fine. Almost there. Wake up.'

The Kathleen Mary

Mara stirred. She spoke faintly; I had to put my ear right next to her mouth to hear what she said. 'Turn the boat. Let the wind out of the sail. Slower.'

I moved the tiller and the sail flapped. I loosened the sheet. Yes, I knew what to do. Take down the mainsail; get the oars out. The sail tumbled down and the boom swung round and nearly knocked Mara. The boat rocked horribly.

I stared out into the dark toward where the lights were moving.

'Hello! Anyone?' My voice sounded thin and weak. No one would hear. And maybe they hadn't even seen us: we had no lights.

The sound of an engine starting up echoed across the water.

I waved and shouted.

Django strained forward. He barked.

A voice called out and relief flooded through me. A man's voice, a voice I knew. How could it be possible? But I recognized the boat, now, too: the *Kathleen Mary*. Marek was at the helm.

'Jamie!' Grandpa called out.

'Grandpa!'

The next things happened so fast.

Stardust rocked violently as the waves from the wake of the *Kathleen Mary* rolled under us. Marek cut the engine, brought the boat alongside, and Grandpa reached across the gap to pull the two boats together.

He threw me a rope. 'I'm coming on board.' He stepped across onto our boat. The waves rolled and washed, the boats shuddered. For a sickening moment I thought he'd slip and fall through the gap.

Stardust rocked and lurched. I lost my hold on the tiller. The boat swung round violently.

'Steady.' Grandpa pulled me into a hug with one hand. The other took the tiller and brought the boat round. 'Well done,

Jamie.' He had tears on his face.

I buried my face into his bony chest and let my own tears come.

The boat rocked and swayed and bumped against the fenders of the *Kathleen Mary*.

'Mara's sick,' I gabbled. 'We ran out of water and food.'

Grandpa shouted to Marek for a blanket.

Marek threw one across. He passed Grandpa a flask.

Grandpa wrapped the blanket round Mara. He felt her forehead and her pulse. He picked her up, and passed her across the gap to Marek's waiting arms, as if she weighed almost nothing.

She tried to protest, but only feebly.

'The helicopter sent the message you'd been spotted. The lifeboat's on its way,' Grandpa said. 'I'll sail *Stardust* back for you.'

Mara would be mad with herself for getting sick and not sailing her own boat home. I'd be a very poor substitute, but at least one of us would bring *Stardust* safely back.

'I'll sail with you,' I said. 'Me and Django.'

'We'll sail her together,' Grandpa said.

The lifeboat roared across the bay: the inflatable RIB, with full crew and medical kit and everything. They took Mara on board, and they talked to Grandpa and Marek and off they sped again.

Grandpa untied the rope.

Marek motored slowly towards our island in the *Kathleen Mary*.

Grandpa and I set the sails on *Stardust* and together we sailed the last few kilometres back to shore.

'What are all those lights on the beach?' I said. 'And that massive bonfire!'

'Word's got out that you're found and safe,' Grandpa said. 'Everyone's come down with torches to see you safely home.' He was properly crying now. 'Oh, Jamie.' He choked on his words. 'But it was a terrible, terrible thing you put us through. Your grandma and your dad and your sister . . . we thought . . . we feared . . . ' He couldn't say the words.

But I knew. Dead and drowned, that's what they'd thought.

'Your mum was extraordinary, Jamie. She said you were alive, she said she knew, she felt it in her bones. She kept faith that we'd find you on some remote island, making a fire and having some adventure . . . '

Grandpa rowed the last few metres onto the beach. I was too exhausted even to lift an oar.

I untied Django. He barked and barked.

Mum and Dad were already wading out through the shallow water, reaching out, lifting me off the boat together and carrying me onto the sand.

Everyone cheered and waved.

Part Three:
Afterwards

Home

That's all I remember. I slept and slept, they told me afterwards. Two whole days of sleeping. The doctor came. I needed fluids and rest, and I'd be perfectly fine.

Mara needed much more time to recover. The hospital put her on a drip. She was malnourished, they discovered, as well as dehydrated. She needed a lot more care. She'd not be starting school.

I told Mum everything. I told her all the things I should have said before, about the way Mara lived, about her mother barely looking after her, about her needing to see her dad.

Mum listened, and nodded. She told me not to worry. She said she'd go and see Mara's mother herself. Everyone was beginning

to understand that Mara's mum needed help. She'd been struggling alone and unwell for much too long. She needed friends
and neighbours, but more than that. Proper medical care, coun-
selling.

I tried to say sorry for what we'd done. Sorry for the worry
and the grief and the heartache.

Mum kept looking at me. Touching my arm as she went past,
as if to check I was really there.

It was teatime, three days later. Everyone was sitting round
the kitchen table: Mum and Dad and Fee and Granny and
Grandpa. I finally told my story of how it all happened.

Fee rolled her eyes. 'Typical,' she kept saying. 'That girl's
totally crazy.'

Granny tutted.

Mum kept making more tea.

No one could believe we had done all those things for real.
They thought I'd made up the dolphins, too.

'And what was it all for?' Dad said. 'That's what I don't understand.'

'I didn't mean to go to sea. It was a total accident, to start with,' I said. 'But Mara was making a point. A protest.'

I tried to explain about Mara and school and her dad. 'She needs to see him,' I said. 'She misses him. It can't be right, that her mum doesn't let her see him or even write to him. Mara wanted to show her mum—show everyone—that she can't bear to be sent away to school. She needs her freedom, to be outside. She will shrivel and die if they make her go. She isn't like anyone else. There has to be another way.'

Grandpa said he was to blame. 'Everyone on the island should feel responsible,' he said. 'Mara's mother could not look after her properly. We all knew that. She could barely look after herself.'

'But you were always kind to Mara,' I said. 'You helped her lots. You shouldn't feel bad.'

'Let's just be happy and grateful that all's well, now,' Mum said. 'Blaming people doesn't help us go forward.'

Django barked.

The back door burst open and Rob and Euan ran in.

Django jumped up, tail wagging.

'You've got a dog!' Rob rubbed Django's wiry body. 'Cool.'

'Not permanently, just till Mara's well,' Mum said.

'You could have one of our new collie pups,' Euan said. 'We've got five, born the night before last.'

'And you're famous,' Rob said. 'You were on the radio and the telly and on the internet and everything.'

'Tea, boys?' Mum said.

'Nah, thanks, Mrs Mackinnon.'

'Cake, then.' Granny cut two big slabs of sponge cake with jam in the middle. They scoffed it down.

'School starts on Tuesday,' Rob said. 'You'll be well popular. Like, a hero.'

Dad frowned. 'Or a lesson in What *Not* to Do.'

Grandpa put his hand on my shoulder. 'He did pretty well. He's sailed a twelve-foot boat to St Kilda and back, which is more than most people his age. Any age, for that matter. I'm proud of you, Jamie Mackinnon.'

I blinked back tears. No way I wanted Rob and Euan to see that. But weirdly, everyone seemed to be doing the same.

Mum jumped up and went to the stove. 'I'll fill the kettle. More tea anyone?'

Everyone laughed.

'We're swimming in tea, Kath,' Dad said. He went to put his arms around her and they danced close together, a step or two.

'This family!' Fee rolled her eyes.

'This family's the BEST,' I said, and that made Mum cry all over again.

So that was my wild adventure, our first island summer. School started up. I was a hero for a week or so. People forgot about it all soon enough. Mara stayed in hospital for ages. People on the island made efforts to be friendly with her mum. We'd see her out and about more often. Mum told her about a job coming up at the Fisheries.

I cycled over to see Mara when she was finally let out of hospital. She was sitting in her garden under the rowan tree. She was still thin, but she looked taller, older. It was odd, talking to her there instead of on a beach or the boat. Strange, after all that had happened.

Django jumped up to greet me.

'It was lovely having him at ours,' I told her. 'We're going to get one of Rob's sheepdog puppies.'

'That's good,' Mara said. 'Choose the one that's happiest and friendliest. I'll come with you to choose, if you like.'

'It's OK,' I said. 'I've already chosen one. She's black with a white ear and paws and a white patch on her forehead.'

'What will you call her?'

'Bonny,' I said. 'Or maybe Stardust, Dusty for short.'

Mara smiled. 'After my boat!'

'Kind of.'

We were both quiet for a while. Django settled down between us.

'I had a tutor in the hospital,' Mara said. 'And I'm going to have one visit me here. Just mornings, three times a week to start with. And guess what? I've had a letter from my dad.'

'Wow,' I said. 'That's awesome.'

She laughed. 'When I was so ill, Mum realized she had to tell him what had happened. He sent me a card. I wrote back. I might be allowed to visit him.'

'You got what you wanted. You were right to sail away!'

'Of course I was.'

'I'm glad I sailed with you.'

The next few weeks, I'd be coming home from school or out in the yard at lunchtime with Rob and Euan and Wren, and we'd see Mara out in the bay, sailing *Stardust*, just like before.

After school most afternoons I'd spend an hour or more with

Grandpa in the boat shed, and sometimes we talked about her. Grandpa missed her. She'd stopped coming to the shed. But I was learning fast, Grandpa said. I'd got much more confident. I was learning to be patient. To not give up when things seemed difficult. What Grandpa called *doggedness*. 'It's that quality which makes all the difference,' he said.

'We'll make a boatbuilder of you yet, Jamie.'

That made me proud. I was learning the skills that my family had practised for generations, making beautiful boats, learning how to live and be happy on our island.

I'd make a boat of my own, one day. I'd sail it out in the bay. I'd sail to the fishing islands, and maybe all the way to St Kilda. I'd remember the very first time I saw Mara, that first summer morning.

She went away to visit her dad, like she said she would. She didn't say goodbye. I should have been used to that, but I missed her all the same.

In spring the next year, a postcard arrived for me with a Portuguese stamp and a picture of a sunny fishing village.

Dear Jamie

This is the place I told you about. Today is Saturday and I'm sitting on the sunny terrace under the vine. My grandmother's cooking lunch. Papai's out in the boat, fishing. He recognized me at the airport so you were right about that: I am not so different from when I was 7, just taller and stronger. I have to go to school, mornings only, and it isn't too bad, except I still can't speak much Portuguese. I understand more than I can speak. Papai says if I go to school I can get a good job one day and earn enough money to buy a bigger boat for my trip across the Atlantic. He says Portuguese people have a history of going to sea and having adventures. When I find my own paradise island I will send you a message in a bottle. Give Bonny/Dusty a hug from me. Keep sailing. Sing your own song.

Mara X

CARD

PORTUGAL 3.50

JAMIE MACKINNON

C/O THE BOATHOUSE

NORTH ISLAND,

OUTER HEBRIDES, UK

Acknowledgements

This is a work of fiction. I have changed details and invented places to suit my story. I'd like to thank Nicola Davies for sharing many happy experiences on the islands of the Outer Hebrides. I am grateful to Bath Spa University for funding one of my research trips to North Uist and Grimsay. Thank you to my inspiring editor, Liz Cross, to Helen Crawford-White for her beautiful cover image, and to everyone in the children's books team at Oxford University Press.

Julia Green

Julia Green lives in Bath, but her favourite places are wild remote islands, beaches, cliffs and hilltops. She has spent many happy times on the islands of the Outer Hebrides. She has two grown-up sons who inspire her with their wild spirit of adventure. One of them recently sailed with a friend in a small boat across the Atlantic ocean, through the Panama Canal and across the Pacific ocean, and lived for six months on a tiny island. Julia is the Course Director for the MA Writing for Young People at Bath Spa University, which has launched the careers of many children's authors. She has written more than seventeen books for children and young adults.

You can find out more about Julia on her website
www.julia-green.co.uk
Visit her author page on Facebook **@JuliaGreenAuthor**
Follow her on Twitter **@JGreenAuthor**

Also by
Julia Green

Turn the page to read an extract.

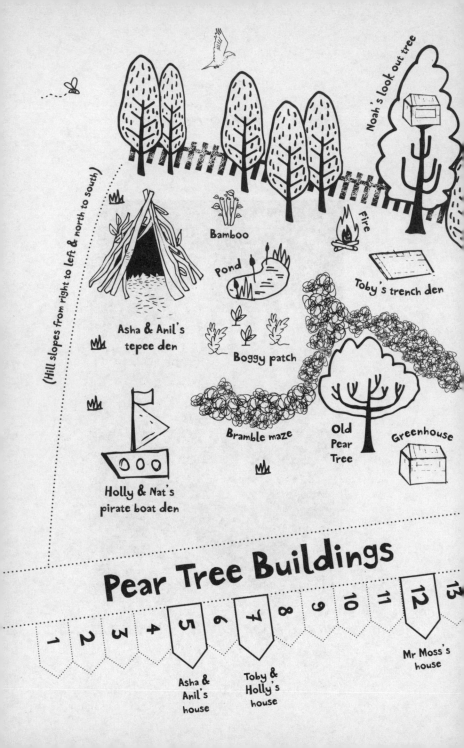

(Hill slopes from right to left & north to south)

Noah's look out tree

Bamboo

Fire

Pond

Toby's trench den

Asha & Anil's tepee den

Boggy patch

Bramble maze

Old Pear Tree

Greenhouse

Holly & Nat's pirate boat den

Pear Tree Buildings

1 2 3 4 5 6 7 8 9 10 11 12 13

Asha & Anil's house

Toby & Holly's house

Mr Moss's house

The Wilderness

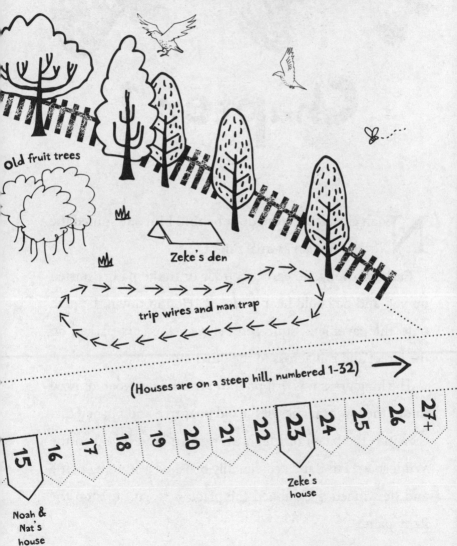

Old fruit trees

Zeke's den

trip wires and man trap

(Houses are on a steep hill, numbered 1-32) →

15 16 17 18 19 20 21 22 23 24 25 26 27+

Noah & Nat's house

Zeke's house

Chapter 1

Noah closed the front door behind him. He sniffed the air, the way an animal might.

Early morning. So early, the roar of traffic hadn't started up yet, and he could hear birdsong. He ran down the path onto the pavement, squeezed between the cars parked on the street and ran across to the other side.

The long grass was dripping wet from dew. Noah ducked under the low branches of the old pear tree and pushed further into the patch of rough overgrown land he called the Wilderness. His hand accidentally brushed a stinging nettle and he winced. He rubbed the place with spit to stop the itchy pain.

Ahead of him in the deep shadow under the trees something moved.

Noah crouched down behind the net of brambles to watch. The hair on the back of his neck bristled.

What was it?

Something bigger than a fox. Not a person.

His heart thudded. He watched, and waited.

A deer stepped out of the shadows into a pool of sunlight.

Noah blinked, to be sure it was really there.

Slanting sunlight spilled through the green canopy of trees at the bottom of the Wilderness. The deer stood completely still, a dark shape silhouetted against the light. It stared directly at Noah.

He saw the way its sides heaved slightly as it breathed in and out, as if it had been running. He saw the deep pools of its eyes, and the furry edges of its ears, and its breath rising like steam. It was a young deer: Noah could make out two small antlers, stubby growths that one day would be big and forked, like branches.

They looked at each other, deer and boy: a moment that felt like recognition, as if something had passed between them.

Noah's own breath steadied and slowed. He blinked.

And in that second, the deer had gone. Disappeared totally, as if it had dissolved into nothing in the warming air, leaving no trace.

How had it even been there in the first place?

Already, Noah began to doubt himself.

And yet it had seemed so real . . . as if he could have reached out his hand, and touched its warm fur.

Even so, he wouldn't tell the others about the deer. Not yet. Just in case it hadn't really been there at all.

Ready for more great stories?
You might like these . . .